The
Christmas
Pickle

The Christmas Pickle

A Christmas Folktale
Dedicated to all those who have wondered,
"Why is there a pickle on our Christmas tree?"

Judy Lee Aguiar

Turnapaige & Reed Moore
A Publishing Company

The Christmas Pickle

Library of Congress Control Number 2002094900

ISBN 0-9725231-0-3

First Edition, December 2002

Cover Design: Tom Rodriguez, TJR Designs

Cover & Author Photographs: Marianne Beams DeLuca.

Interior Art: Most of the images in this book were sourced from copyrighted clipart from the following and are used with permission granted through their respective License Agreements:

• *Art Explosion* from Nova Development, 23801 Calabasas Road, Suite 2005, Calabasas, CA 91302.

• *DeskGallery Mega-Bundle* from Zedcor, Inc., 3420 N. Dodge Blvd., Suite Z, Tucson, AZ 85716.

• *Print Perfect* from Cosmi Corporation, 2600 Homestead Place, Rancho Dominguez, CA 90220.

Turnapaige & Reed Moore
A Publishing Company
P.O. Box 412, Scottsdale, Arizona 85252

Dedicated

To all those who have wondered,
"Why is there a pickle on our Christmas tree?"

Table of Contents

*W*hile owning and working in a Christmas store these past twenty years, I've been introduced to some wonderful Christmas traditions from all over the world. One of the most delightful and amusing is the tradition of the Christmas Pickle.

The tradition of hiding the Christmas Pickle on the Christmas tree has its roots in Prussian history and is fast becoming an American favorite. In our store, out of literally thousands of ornaments and hundreds of designs, the pickle ornament is consistently the top selling ornament every year!

It's wonderful to see so many people adding new traditions to their Christmas celebrations, and the Christmas Pickle is one that everyone can enjoy. I have seen families come in to buy their very first pickle ornament and through the years as their children grow, I've seen them return to select smaller, more discreet pickles—making the pickle even more difficult to find on the Christmas tree.

Although many people are aware of the tradition of the Christmas Pickle, few know the legend behind the tradition. This book tells the story of how the tradition of the Christmas Pickle began.

I hope that you enjoy this folktale and if you do not already take part in the tradition, I hope that you decide to make the tradition of the Christmas Pickle a part of your annual Christmas celebration.

Merry Christmas to you, your family, and friends—and best wishes for years to come.

Judy Lee Aguiar

Acknowledgements

Many people helped make this book possible.

I would like to thank

My husband: Manuel Aguiar,

My mother and father: Margrit and Arthur Maasch, and

My sister: Janny Webb

For their love, patience, inspiration, and encouragement.

I would like to specially thank my friend, Marianne Beams DeLuca

For her expertise in both editing and photography.

I would also like to thank my friends:

Liegha Crump and Sandy Dingler Stewart

For their diligence in editing and proofreading,

In addition, I would like to thank the rest of my family and friends

Who have supported and advised me during this process.

I sincerely thank all of you for your love, friendship, and assistance.

'God Bless You All and Merry Christmas!

Most often it is—the Littlest things,
That to our soul—the Greatest joy brings.

Our memories hold fast—and steadily cling,
To family traditions—that make our hearts sing.

—JLA

*T*he new snow that dusted the trees and tiled rooftops glistened with the encroaching rays of the morning sun in the Prussian Kingdom of Vlassika. It was Christmas time and the smell of fresh-baked pastries and the wooded scent of pine floated above the Kingdom, drifting in the morning fog. King Frederick stood on his balcony overlooking the many small villages that spread out in all directions from his palace. He inhaled deeply and enjoyed the morning with all his senses. Quietly, Queen Margarete came and stood behind him. "It is a beautiful morning!" she softly exclaimed.

"Yes," he replied, "and this Christmas will be the best ever!" He put his arm around Queen Margarete's waist and pulled her close.

"Since you made the announcement, you seem much more at ease," she whispered happily.

"I am. Just the prospect that what we propose will ensure that the Kingdom is secure and happy for well into the future, makes me feel like a great weight has been lifted from my heart."

Queen Margarete rested her head against his shoulder. "The contest begins this afternoon. Many courtiers have arrived in the last few days. I'm sure that there will be one that will satisfy our needs."

They held each other close and watched the sun rise over the great Kingdom.

"We had best get ready—the court awaits and we have much to do today. I'll ring for our servants." Queen Margarete kissed her King and hurried off to find her handmaids.

King Frederick lingered a bit longer, took another deep breath, and whispered under his breath, "Let the contest begin."

The palace bustled with excitement and anticipation. Courtiers and royalty from across the land filled the palace. In the afternoon, they began lining the hallways and crowding the stairs. When the court attendants opened the doors to the great hall, the awaiting crowd cheered with delight and streamed through the doors to fill the room from wall-to-wall. As King Frederick and Queen Margarete entered the room, they all bowed and curtsied with respect.

"Welcome! Welcome!" announced King Frederick. "We welcome our royal friends, noblemen, fellow countrymen, and ladies of the court. We welcome you to this joyous occasion."

The King continued, "As you are aware, today begins the royal competition. Before we begin, we would like to remind you that those who wish to enter must be between the ages of 19 and 25 years old and a royal sponsor must present you to the court. If you wish to enter, please come forward with your sponsor and give your name to the royal registrar."

One-by-one the contestants approached with their sponsors. As the last nobleman signed his name, the registrar closed his book. He looked to the King and was about to speak when suddenly a woman's voice interrupted him, "Excuse me, kind sir. There is one more contestant who wishes to register."

The registrar looked toward she who spoke. A young and beautiful maiden curtsied before him.

"Well, where is this contestant? " queried the registrar.

"Kind sir, it is I who wishes to register," answered the maiden.

A murmur traveled through the great hall. The King quickly dispelled the murmurs when he asked the young maiden, "My lady, you do understand that this is a contest to become an heir to our throne?"

"Yes, my King. I do understand," she answered respectfully bowing before the throne.

King Frederick was perplexed and looked to his Queen. She gave him a look that confused him even more. He cleared his throat and continued, "My dear, you do know that to enter this contest you must have a royal sponsor."

"Yes, my King. I do have a sponsor," she looked up at him through her long dark lashes.

"You do have a sponsor," he said almost to himself. "Ah yes, you do have a sponsor—May we inquire whom your sponsor is?"

"Yes, my King. I am honored that Her Royal Highness, the Queen, has chosen to be my sponsor."

"Her Royal Highness, the Queen," he muttered to himself. "The Queen?" he exclaimed with surprise. He looked at Queen Margarete who raised her eyebrows and smiled playfully at him.

"It is true. I am her sponsor," Queen Margarete announced. "I have known Petra since she was born and it has been a joy to have her near— to hear her laugh and sing, to watch her dance and play, and to see her grow into the beautiful and intelligent young lady you see before you today. It is my sincere pleasure to present to the court, Petra, first-born daughter of Sir Nicholas and my lady-in-waiting, Lady Karolina."

"But, my dear Queen," the King whispered to her.

"You will not suggest," she whispered smartly, "that because she is a maiden that she is not capable of ruling the Kingdom?"

King Frederick knew that if he were to pursue this any further, he would not be in any great favor with his Queen. He quickly turned to his registrar and stated, "Open your book. You have another contestant to enter." He glanced at Queen Margarete, who was smiling favorably at the young maiden, Petra, as she signed her name in the registrar's book.

When Petra finished signing her name, the registrar looked up over his spectacles and asked, "Is there anyone else?"

A few chuckles echoed in the great hall, but no one else came forward.

The registrar, satisficd that he had recorded all the contest entries, closed the book and presented it to King Frederick. "My lord, the list of contestants. By my count, there are one hundred and sixteen contestants."

"Excellent!" exclaimed King Frederick. "Now, to the competition." King Frederick made himself comfortable on his throne with Queen Margarete at his side. "The contest will begin tomorrow morning— but you may start making preparations immediately following this assembly."

A rumbling of whispers circulated throughout the hall.

King Frederick continued, "Each of you are to go out into the Kingdom, accompanied only by a minimal escort. Somewhere in one of the Kingdom's villages, there lives an ornament maker. This ornament maker is not well-known, but it is claimed that he makes the most wonderful ornaments for the Christmas tree—and he makes them entirely of glass."

The sound of awe filled the great hall.

"When you find this ornament maker, you are to choose an ornament and bring it back to decorate the Christmas tree here in the palace. You will have exactly five days to make your journey, find the ornament maker, and return with your ornament on Christmas Eve." King Frederick paused and looked to his Queen.

Queen Margarete then spoke. "Remember, you are to accomplish this task without any assistance from anyone at court. Once the contest begins, you are completely on your own. If you seek advice or receive help from anyone at court, you will be disqualified."

"Yes," interjected King Frederick, "and we have posted several contest officials throughout each village to ensure that all contestants comply with all the rules of the contest." King Frederick paused and then continued. "When all of you have returned on Christmas Eve, we will gather in the great hall around the Christmas tree and each of you will make your presentations."

Queen Margarete added, "As part of your presentation, we also expect you to tell us how you found the ornament maker and what you have encountered during your quest."

"After all the presentations have been made, Queen

Margarete and I will determine the winner of the contest, who will be the heir to our throne, and future King...or Queen." He quickly corrected. He stifled a laugh as he looked to his Queen He paused for a moment in thought and then asked, "Are there any questions?"

The hall filled with excitement and anticipation. Voices hesitantly rose from silence to whispers and people shifted from one place to another as they discussed the King's announcement. Finally, a young gentleman stepped forward, bowed, and spoke, "Sire, I have a question."

"Present yourself and state your question," King Frederick answered.

"I am Sir Norbert, son of Count Seewald. If it will please your Highness, can you tell us how you will determine the winner of the contest? Will it be by how quickly we return with the ornament, the beauty of the ornament, or the means by which we accomplished our task?"

"Excellent question, Sir Norbert. I assure you that we will consider all things. We will not take the decision lightly; after all, the contest winner must be able to reign as regent over our great and wonderful Kingdom. We urge you to be on your best behavior and use good judgment. Are there any other questions?"

The whispers began once more, but no one stepped forward. "Well then, to the preparations—and I sincerely wish you all farewell. We will see you all on Christmas Eve!" King Frederick cheered. Then he and Queen Margarete left the great hall followed by the noblemen and women. Some of the contestants lingered, but soon all had left the great hall. The palace and the palace grounds were alive with excitement. There was a great commotion as the eager contestants made preparations to leave.

Because Petra didn't know how to ride horseback, she had to travel by carriage. She had arranged to take only one coachman to accompany her. Everyone was aghast that she had decided not to have her Governess accompany her. After all, she was a maiden and it was expected, but Petra did not want to take more of an escort than any of the male contestants did. In the end, her parents and Governess gave consent and for safety's sake, Petra asked her Godfather to accompany her as coachman.

Petra worked late into the night. She had much to do. She didn't want to forget a single thing, but she also didn't want to over-pack. Petra checked and rechecked the items that she packed. She had to travel light, but she had to have the necessities for the next four or five days. After all, she would not be able to send back to the palace for anything without risking disqualification.

As the bells in the village below proclaimed the midnight hour, Petra blew out the candles in her room, slipped under her feathery covers, and tried desperately to sleep. Outside, a light snow drifted down— anticipation and excitement made for a fitful sleep, but non-the-less…she slept.

Chapter Two

*P*etra awoke with a start. Her heart was pounding. *"What time is it? Am I late? Has everyone gone? Am I the last to leave?"*

She bolted out of bed and drew back the curtains to look out at the courtyard. The sky was just beginning to shimmer with the first light of day.

She wasn't late, but there were already several horses being prepared in the courtyard. She quickly dressed and went down the hall to awaken her Governess.

Downstairs in the courtyard, things really began to stir. The horses had to be fed, saddled, and packed. Squires and stable hands hurried back and forth carrying supplies. Soon hundreds of horses and men filled the

courtyard. What a noise they all made!

After awaking her Governess, Petra ate a light breakfast and then hurried to find her Godfather to help him with their carriage. Their carriage stood at the north end of the courtyard. Her Godfather was busy tending the horses: checking their harnesses and horseshoes while the horses leisurely ate their oats.

"Good morning, Godfather," Petra called cheerily. She shivered as she noticed her breath coming out in visible puffs in the cold morning air.

"Good Morning, Sweetheart," her Godfather called back.

"Are we ready to start loading the carriage?"

"We're ready." Petra's Godfather looked around for a moment and then motioned to a young boy, "Gerhart! Come here and help Mistress Petra with her things."

Petra led Gerhart to her quarters. Gerhart picked up as many bags as he could possibly carry (five bags to be exact) and

headed back down to the courtyard. Petra stood with her hands on her hips while she thought. There were still three bags and a small lacquered-wood box left to carry. *"I could do it,"* she thought defiantly. She waited for a few seconds and then anxiety took over. She grabbed two of the bags with one hand, clutched the box under her other arm, grabbed the last bag, and headed downstairs. She heard her Governess shriek with dismay before she even saw her at the foot of the stairs.

"Mistress Petra! What do you think you are doing? You should not be carrying anything so cumbersome or heavy. Where is that stable boy? How dare he let you carry these things. You are not a peasant girl…"

Petra met her Governess in the middle of the stairs. "It's alright," she soothed. "I can manage. I may have to carry much more during my travels. After all, this is not a pleasure trip."

Petra's Governess sighed deeply while stepping aside. "Petra, just don't over do it. Remember, you are still a Lady and a member of the royal court."

"Don't worry…" Petra smiled and hurried out into the courtyard to her carriage.

Petra made it to the carriage and everything was packed and stowed. Petra hugged her family and friends 'Good bye,' wiped away a few tears, and excitedly climbed in the carriage. The gates of the courtyard were opened with great fanfare and contestants filed out the gate.

How exciting it was. People cheering and waving, the horses parading gallantly, the courtiers poised and perfect, the trumpets blaring—it was all quite grand.

Petra could hardly sit still in the carriage. As they left the palace grounds, Petra leaned out the window in anticipation. Several contestants came by her carriage window to meet her and to wish her luck. As they came to open road, the group began to disperse as many of the horsemen took off in a wild gallop. Petra watched as many of the horses passed by, and then she called out, "Godfather! Will we be able to go any faster? They're all leaving us behind!"

"I'll see what I can do," he answered. "Hold on tight!"

Petra heard the crack of a whip and felt the carriage pitch forward. She could hear the horses fall into a gallop. They were

well on their way to the first village—in fact, she could see it in the near distance. The village of Gurkenheim was normally a good hour's ride from the palace, but at the speed they were going, she estimated that they would be there in less than 30 minutes.

Petra was clinging on tightly to the inner railing of the carriage. It felt good—she seemed to have so much energy built up inside her and gripping the railing made her feel as though she was doing something. She was feeling somewhat powerless. To help make the time pass a little easier, she began to reformulate her plans to find the ornament maker. She repeatedly went over her plans and her checklist—she became quite preoccupied.

She figured that the best place to start her search would be at the center of the Kingdom. Dillsburg was not only the centermost village of the Kingdom, but it was the largest of all the villages in Vlassika. Dillsburg had the most businesses and officials, and she knew that from Dillsburg, she could quickly and easily get to all the other villages.

Petra fumbled with her cloak and gloves. *"Let's see…if Gurkenheim is usually one hour away and it's taking us half the time,"* she began to calculate, *"and Dillsburg is approximately four hours from Gurkenheim…"* She continued to figure, occasionally stopping to watch the scenery as it changed from the hillside heights of the palace grounds to the valley of the villages.

She noticed that the light snow they had that night didn't seem to leave much on the ground as they entered the

valley, and it seemed much warmer. Petra continued her calculations, *"What was it again? Dillsburg is approximately 4 hours from Gurkenheim... plus the time it will take to go through Gurkenheim. We should almost—"* Petra was doing the math in her head when suddenly the carriage careened to the left. There was a huge jolt, and she heard something snap and then crack.

Petra clung on for dear life and yet her head hit the roof of the carriage. There was a terrible noise and rumbling beneath her. The carriage came to a sudden stop and almost tipped completely on its side. The horses complained loudly and she could hear her Godfather shouting.

Petra was stunned and very shaken. She rubbed the top of her head and looked out the window to see what had happened. Villagers were rushing toward them. Someone she didn't know helped her out of the leaning carriage. "Mistress, are you hurt?" the stranger asked.

"What happened?" Petra asked the stranger.

"The back axle of your carriage snapped. You're lucky that no one was seriously injured! Are you hurt?" the stranger again inquired.

"I'm fine. Where is my Godfather? Is he alright?"

"There he is. He seems in good health," the stranger answered.

"Godfather!" Petra called as she rushed to his side.

"Petra, are you well?" her Godfather asked.

"Yes. Yes. I'm well. Are you?"

"Yes, but I'm afraid our transportation is not. We're going to need a new carriage or a least a wheelwright to make repairs." Petra's Godfather turned to some of the villagers and asked, "Is there a wheelwright in the village?"

One of the villagers stepped up, "Yes, he's at the center square. You can't miss it—there's a large wagon wheel suspended above the door of his workshop. He gets lots of business this time of year. Potholes—they're a real problem on this road. Someone should do something."

Petra looked around. She was still a bit dazed and confused. Just then, the same stranger approached her again. "Mistress. May I help you with your things or perhaps give you a ride to the village center?"

"Well, I suppose…" Petra looked at the stranger. He was a handsome young man dressed in fine clothing. "My name is Petra. Should I know you, kind sir?"

The young man blushed with embarrassment. "Dear Lady, forgive me. My manners…with the accident…I …I am Sir Manfred. I am at your service, Mistress." He bowed before her.

Petra smiled, "Sir Manfred. It is a pleasure meeting you. Thank you for your offer of assistance. Are you by any chance also a contestant?"

"Yes Mistress, I too am a contestant."

"And you have stopped to offer me assistance? You are a true gentleman."

Sir Manfred blushed slightly.

"Thank you for your offer, but seeing that you are also a contestant, I cannot detain you from your quest. I must deal with this mishap on my own and you must continue on your way. "

"Mistress…?"

"Please, call me Petra."

Sir Manfred looked as though she had given him a gift. "Mistress Petra," he repeated with pride, " I cannot continue on my quest knowing that I had left you here. Please allow me to do something."

"No. I must do this myself. You must take me seriously and treat me as a competitor. I truly appreciate your offer and I am impressed with your noble manner. I trust I will see you again at the end of the quest when we make our presentations."

"I wish you would allow me to help you, but I do not wish to insult you. Therefore, I will do as you wish. I will continue on my way, but I will alert the wheelwright in the village to let him know that you are need of assistance. I will see you Christmas Eve." Sir Manfred mounted his horse, "Farewell, Mistress Petra."

Petra felt herself blushing, "Farewell, Sir Manfred."

After Sir Manfred rode off, Petra cleared her mind and set to the matter at hand. She secured transportation into the village for herself, her Godfather, and their belongings. Sir Manfred had indeed alerted the wheelwright, and he was already preparing to get their carriage and horses and bring them back for repair.

"How long will it take to repair the carriage?" Petra asked the wheelwright.

"It depends on the damage. Could be two to three days, four at the most," the wheelwright answered.

"Four days!" Petra shrieked. "The contest only lasts five days. I can't be delayed for four days! Do you have an extra carriage that I may borrow?"

"Well, I normally have an extra carriage, but the baker is currently using that carriage."

"The baker?"

"Last week, the baker's carriage had an accident. Just about the same place where you did. The baker's wife broke her arm." The wheelwright shook his head, "The potholes are bad this time of year. Someone really should do something."

"Perhaps, I can borrow the carriage from the baker. Where can I find the bakery?"

"It's directly across the square. Just follow your nose. They make the finest bread and pastries in the Kingdom. You can smell the yeast and sweet spices from here."

Chapter Three

*P*etra looked across the square in the direction the
wheelwright motioned. A sign resembling a large pretzel
hung above one of the shops. She thanked the
wheelwright and quickly made her way across the square. *"The
wheelwright had spoken truly,"* she mused. *"The smell is
almost irresistible!"*

As she neared the bakery, she could see the baker loading
his carriage with baskets of freshly baked breads and boxes of
confections. The warm sweet smell nearly overwhelmed her and
made her mouth water in desire.

She swallowed hard before presenting herself to the
baker, who bowed deeply in her presence. Petra curtsied politely
in reply and asked, "Kind Sir, I am Mistress Petra. The
wheelwright across the square directed me to you. Are you the
baker, Sir?"

"Yes, Mistress. I am the baker," he said with another
bow. "I am Master Zucker. How may I be of assistance?"

"It is a pleasure to make your acquaintance, Master Zucker. I am on a royal quest, and during this quest, the axle on my carriage broke upon entering Gurkenheim…"

"Ah yes, those potholes are very bad this time of year. Someone really should do something," the baker interjected sympathetically. "My wife had an accident just last week and she broke her arm, poor thing. Are you well, Mistress?"

"Yes, yes I am. Thank you. However, my quest…the wheelwright told me that he has lent you this carriage until he completes repairs on your carriage. I was wondering if you could delay your deliveries and allow me to borrow your carriage for my quest. I would be willing to compensate you."

"Well, I would love to assist you Mistress, but as you can see I am preparing to make my deliveries now. I am already several days behind due to the accident…my poor wife. Normally, she would be here; tending the bakery while I am away, but she cannot because of her arm. I must close our bakery until I return. In addition, I must make these deliveries to the village of Heinzinger, or we will not receive our shipment of grain. I am sorry, but I could lend you the carriage when I return in two days."

Petra bit her lip and fought back her tears. *"Even two days is too long. I can't stay in Gurkenheim for two days!"*

She suffered silently. Suddenly, she had a thought that brightened her expression. "What if I agreed to make those deliveries for you?"

"I could not possible burden you, dear Mistress, with a menial task such as that! It's simply not proper."

"It would be no burden and it certainly is not improper to offer my services in exchange for the use of your carriage. I believe it to be an excellent solution. Your bakery could remain open, your grain deliveries would be assured, and I will have the transportation I need to continue on my quest. Do you agree?"

The baker thought for a moment. He looked back at his storefront and carefully considered her offer. He saw the look of pleading desperation on Petra's face and crumbled at her resolve. "Yes, Mistress. I agree."

Petra nearly squealed with delight. The baker had to laugh at her enthusiasm. "The families in Heinzinger will certainly have a shock to have someone as refined as you delivering their baked goods. They'll think I've gone mad."

"Let me go tell my Godfather and have our travel bags loaded. I'll be back momentarily."

"I'll finish loading the baked goods. It might be a bit crowded. Are you sure you wish to do this?"

"Yes, yes. Be sure you prepare instructions for me as to where I am to deliver your delectable pastries and confections. I want to insure that I deliver everything correctly," Petra directed. "Please excuse me. I must take leave to find my Godfather. I will return shortly," she called out as she hurried back across the square.

Petra found her Godfather and had all their things delivered and loaded on the baker's carriage. She thanked the baker for his kindness and indulgence. Master Zucker gave Petra the instructions for the deliveries and the baker's wife presented Petra with a basket of sandwiches, pastries, confections, and beverages for her and her Godfather to enjoy on their travels.

"How thoughtful!" Petra exclaimed. "Thank you very much." She set the basket in the carriage and then turned to them, " If you please, I have one other question before we take our leave."

"Yes, Mistress?" the baker's wife asked with interest.

"Do either of you know of an ornament maker in this or any other village of Vlassika that makes Christmas ornaments out of glass?"

The baker and his wife looked at each other for an answer. Finally, they both shook their heads and the baker replied, "No, Mistress. I am sorry, but I have not heard of any. Perhaps someone in Heinzinger will know."

Petra extended her hand in gratitude, "Thank you again for your troubles and I wish you both a very Merry Christmas."

"Thank you, Mistress. Merry Christmas to you and fare well on your quest," the baker replied taking her hand.

"Farewell, Mistress," the baker's wife called out as the

carriage loaded with breads and pastries lurched forward. Petra waved goodbye and the carriage left the village square and turned down the road heading eastward to Heinzinger.

Petra settled back into the carriage seat. She sat facing the back of the carriage. As she looked out the window, she saw Gurkenheim disappearing in the distance.

All around her, the carriage was stacked with baskets of freshly baked breads, buns, rolls, and pretzels; and boxes of

cakes, whipped cream pastries, cookies, and confections. She barely had room to move. The scent of all the food was overpowering.

The day had worn on and Petra was famished. She eyed the basket of treats from the baker's wife and she decided to give in to her hunger. It was much warmer and she removed her gloves and cloak. She dug into the basket and retrieved a

sandwich and a beverage. She laid out a napkin on her lap and suddenly lapsed into guilt.

She banged on the carriage wall and called out, "Godfather! Are you hungry? Would you like a sandwich and something warm to drink?"

"No thank you, dear heart," he replied looking into the carriage from a small window above. "I've already eaten a sandwich your Godmother prepared and packed for me. Go ahead and enjoy. We have a ways to go before we arrive in Heinzinger."

Petra unwrapped a sandwich. *"It certainly looks delicious. I am sooooo hungry,"* she cooed to herself. She took her first bite and rolled her eyes—she couldn't help but moan in delight. She quietly ate her sandwich and she enjoyed every bite as much as the next.

"This bread is so delicious," she remarked to herself. *"Nutty and sweet with a hint of nutmeg and cinnamon. If their pastries are even half as delicious as their bread—I'm sure to gain several pounds in the next two days alone!"*

As she finished her lunch and brushed the few remaining crumbs from her bodice, she turned her mind to her quest. She wiped her hands on her napkin, took a few sips of her tea, and took the baker's instructions and her journal in hand. She glanced over the baker's notes. Then she read her travel plans in her journal.

"This changes everything...but I must remember to ask everyone I meet, if they know the ornament maker...Oh dear," she sighed. *"I forgot to ask the wheelwright. Foolish, foolish girl,"* she scolded herself.

The wheels of the carriage rolled on and the carriage creaked and groaned. Petra was lost in her thoughts as she watched field after field float past her window. The fields were rowed and planted, and in some cases, tiny tips of green were already peaking through the dark crust. They had passed several farmhouses when she realized that they must be in Heinzinger.

Just as she was awakening from her daydreams, Petra's Godfather opened the little window at the top of the carriage. "We're coming to the first stop, Petra. Get your list ready."

"Yes, Godfather. I'm ready." She slipped on her gloves and cloak.

Petra held the list in her hand and made a visual inspection of the things she would leave at their first stop. When the carriage rolled to a stop, she found herself in front of a large and lovely farmhouse. There were crop fields surrounding the house almost as far as Petra could see. As Petra stepped from the carriage, the Lady of the house was there to greet her.

The Lady seemed surprised and stammered as she curtsied before Petra, "Greetings. I'm the Lady of the house. I'm sorry, Mistress, for my appearance. I wasn't expecting company. I had expected..." She paused while smoothing her dress, "I was expecting the baker or his wife from Gurkenheim."

"I have come from Gurkenheim. I am Mistress Petra and I am here as a favor to the baker, Master Zucker, and his wife."

"Oh, welcome Mistress Petra," the Lady of the house replied still flustered. "Let me call some of my children to unburden you. My name is Maria, please won't you come in and warm yourself?"

"Thank you."

Petra followed Maria into the house. Maria gave several orders and word quickly spread throughout the household regarding the "special" delivery of baked goods. Maria's children began to appear one-by-one to meet and greet Petra and to help unload their bakery goods from the carriage.

"You certainly have an impressive farm and lovely children," Petra told Maria.

"Thank you, Mistress," Maria replied smiling. "My family works very hard. We have the largest producing wheat farm in Heinzinger."

"We also grow other crops such as barley, rye, and of course assorted vegetables," she paused shortly. "We have some livestock—though it's difficult to maintain livestock with the wolves coming in from Rellischwald, but wheat is our largest crop."

Even after everything was unloaded, more children still appeared and introduced themselves—twenty-five children to be exact. Petra was overwhelmed. Each child was as pleasant and well groomed as the next, and not all were children—some were full-grown men and women. As she stood meeting each, the Master of the house also appeared and introduced himself.

He bowed with great respect, "Welcome to our home and farm, Mistress. I am Master Tillermann. Are you or your coachman in need of refreshment? How about your horses? Is there anything we can do for you?"

"No, no thank you, kind Sir. We must still make several deliveries and the hour is growing late. But if you might tell me, do any of you know of an ornament maker who makes Christmas ornaments of glass?"

Master Tillermann blinked with surprise, "No, Mistress I do not." He looked to his family and staff. They all shook their heads and no one else answered in reply. "I'm sorry, Mistress. Is there anything else?"

"No thank you, Master Tillermann. I must be on my way." Petra made her way to the door and bid them all a farewell and a Merry Christmas and before she knew it, she was back in the carriage and on her way to the next stop. They made at least six more stops at similar farms—each growing a different type of crop and each with a great number of children. At each stop, she asked the same question, but no one had heard of the ornament maker for whom she sought.

It was beginning to get dark and cold. They had one more stop to make. According to the baker's notes, they were to make their last delivery at the grain miller's house, and they would be able to seek lodging there for the night. Petra looked out her window toward their destination. As the sun slowly sank behind the dark earthy fields, the mill towers darkened against the sky. She sighed with relief and exhaustion—they were almost there.

Their carriage pulled up in front of the grain mill, and the miller (who coincidentally was called Master Mueller), greeted them. He told them that they could make their last delivery and lodge for the night at Mueller's Inn down the road—owned and operated by two of his sons and their wives.

The Inn was quite large, and it was warm, cozy, and clean. Several young boys unloaded the last of the baker's delivery and helped Petra and her Godfather with their baggage to their rooms. "Your carriage and horses will be well cared for," stated the oldest boy. "Have a pleasant stay."

"Thank you very much," Petra responded as she gave the boy some coins for his trouble. Petra went to her room to freshen up after the long day's ride. She wasn't very hungry. All day, in between stops, she had nibbled on an assortment of pastries and cake provided by the baker's wife. Even though she wasn't hungry, she decided that it would be good to go downstairs and share a meal and conversation with the owners of the Inn and the other guests staying for the night.

When she came downstairs, the conversation hushed. Petra really was quite stunning—her dark hair and dark eyes were a startling contrast against her porcelain white skin—and she carried herself with great confidence. The firelight shining on her brought out her fine features and she glowed with the beauty of youth.

Immediately, the gentlemen in the room rose from their seats and offered an open seat to Petra. Petra sat in the seat next to her Godfather. Everyone seemed to be a little nervous and on edge. It seems visitors from the palace were not common at the Inn. Everyone hesitated to speak, let alone continue eating.

Petra noticed and attempted to set them at ease, "Please, please continue as you were. Eat and enjoy. I'm just here to relax, eat a little, and enjoy some conversation with all of you." She smiled an easy smile.

"I'm not sure, Mistress, that you would enjoy much of our conversation. Most of us here are farm owners and we're just talking business. You know boasting and complaining," he smiled apologetically.

A young girl slipped in and served Petra a bowl of winter stew and a plate of fresh bread with butter. Petra smoothed down her napkin, took her spoon in hand, and replied before she took

her first taste, "Sir, it may surprise you, but today I have traveled through a good portion of Heinzinger. I visited quite a few large farms and met their owners as well as their children. I find Heinzinger and their people very enchanting. I would be delighted to hear more regarding the business of farming—that is if you do not consider it an intrusion."

"No, Mistress! You are certainly welcome. I just thought that it might bore you to hear about our trivialities and lamentations." The gentleman smiled at Petra and continued, "Allow me to introduce myself. I am Master Gruenfeld and this is my wife Frieda."

"It's a pleasure to meet you both—all of you. I am Petra and this is my Godfather, Sir Arthur. Thank you for including us in your evening." Petra smiled and raised her glass as a toast to her companions.

 They all drank and then settled down to finish eating. Petra had not been hungry, but the stew and buttered bread was so delicious that she couldn't stop eating it until she had finished every bite and spoonful.

At the table, the conversation soon turned back to the business of farming. Petra didn't understand everything that was discussed, but she did find it interesting that a great deal of their problems involved animals from Rellischwald straying into their fields and destroying crops and livestock. Apparently, just as Maria at the Tillermann's farm had told her about the wolves coming in and killing livestock, other farmers had problems with deer, rabbits, wild pigs, and even bears on occasion. Apparently, the fences that the farmers had been able to construct were sadly inadequate.

Petra chatted with several of the guests and she was sure to ask everyone if they had knowledge of the ornament maker. Several people made suggestions where she might find information in Dillsburg, but no one had ever heard of the ornament maker.

After a while, Petra began feeling the weight of the day. She politely excused herself, said her "Goodnights," and retired to her room. In her room, she changed her clothes and readied herself for bed—making sure that everything was prepared for the next day.

Before going to bed, Petra had one more task left to do. She grabbed the lacquered-wood box and a handsomely bound book that she had brought with her and sat at small writing desk in her room. She carefully opened the delicate box, took out a quill pen and ink, and began writing in her journal. She wrote about everything that had happened, the people she encountered, and the places she had seen. She drew a few maps and she even wrote about the problems that the farmers had discussed at dinner.

When she was finished, she read over her entries, made a few corrections, and thought about the next day. She jotted down a few notes about where to ask for information in Dillsburg and finally, she snuffed out the candle and sunk into bed. She was asleep as soon as she closed her eyes.

Chapter Four

*I*t was morning and Petra lay in bed listening to the movement of people in the hallway and through the stairwell. She knew it would be another long day of traveling, and she was excited about finally getting to Dillsburg to continue on her quest. Oddly, she didn't feel at all regretful about the detour she had taken through Heinzinger. In fact, she felt it had made her trip even more of an adventure.

She got up, dressed, and went downstairs for breakfast. The morning was somewhat uneventful and soon she and her Godfather were packed and on their way to Dillsburg.

The road into Dillsburg was not long and was very well traveled. Petra had much more room in the carriage, since they had delivered all the baked goods, and she was able to sit facing the front of the carriage and the road that lay ahead of them.

They traveled for several hours; passing farm fields in

the quiet of morning. About noon, the scenery changed and the bustling traffic of horses and riders surrounded their carriage— there were crowds of people along the road, and as they entered Dillsburg, it seemed that they could have walked faster than the carriage could carry them through the streets.

Petra stared out of her window. *"Every contestant must*

have come straight here to Dillsburg," Petra thought in disbelief.

Their carriage continued to inch its way down the main street of Dillsburg. Petra became frustrated and anxious. Finally, she rapped on the carriage wall, "Godfather! Why don't you just let me out here? I see a few Inns and places where I might inquire. I'll meet you at the nearest stable."

Petra's Godfather opened his little window, "Wait until I move up a little closer to the walkway. You can't get out here. It's too dangerous."

Petra waited anxiously inside the carriage as they carefully and slowly edged over toward the walkway. When she was finally able to get out, she felt relieved and excited. *"Finally,"* she thought, *"I can seriously begin on my quest!"* Petra arranged a meeting place with her Godfather and she asked him to find a place where they could stay for the night. Soon she was on her way.

There were so many people on the street and in every shop and every Inn—at some places, people literally spilled out onto the street. Between the contestants and their companions alone, it seemed as though nearly the entire Kingdom of Vlassika had descended upon Dillsburg.

Petra had planned to head straight for the nearest official's office to inquire about the ornament maker. Her hopes were quickly dispelled, when upon arriving at the official's office, she learned that all officials were barred from giving any assistance or information regarding the quest.

Petra continued to walk through the crowds, stopping at each shop, and trying to ask everyone she met if they knew the ornament maker. It was very difficult, because most of the people she met were either contestants themselves, companions of the contestants, or court officials in some capacity or another. The few shop owners and residents she did meet were worn and weary of being asked. Some people had taken to wearing hand-made signs saying "I DON'T KNOW" and "DON'T ASK!"

After asking a dozen or so people and seeing so many signs, Petra said decidedly to herself, *"Well, the other contestants may have arrived before me, but they haven't gotten much further."*

A few hours passed. Petra had lunch at one Inn and she had asked dozens and dozens of people ranging from chefs to Inn stewards, butchers, shoemakers, and blacksmiths—everyone she could possibly meet. She had walked quite a distance. She had also

inquired at several Inns if there were any rooms available for the night, and to her dismay, there were none. Her face and feet were cold and she decided it was time to find her Godfather. She hoped that he might have found a place for them to stay. She needed some time to warm up, collect her thoughts, and regroup. She looked to where the stables would be and started to make her way there.

As she headed down the street, she spotted the stables across the way down a narrow side street. As she stepped across a somewhat rough cobblestone road, she was nearly run down by a few careless gentlemen on horses. She heard the clattering of horse hooves—at the last second, a familiar outstretched hand came to her rescue and pulled her to safety. A familiar hand, a familiar figure, face, and voice, "Mistress Petra! What a pleasant surprise."

Petra took his hand tightly and leaned against him still breathless, "Thank you once again, Sir Manfred. It seems you're always there at my rescue."

"Where are you headed? Perhaps, I may escort you there…Oh, excuse me, that is unless you are headed somewhere in regards to the contest," he offered apologetically.

"I'm headed towards the stable to look for my Godfather. I would be delighted if you were to escort me," Petra blushed slightly. "It's simply unbelievable how many people are here. Have they been here since yesterday?"

"Most of them, yes. Did you just arrive today?"

"Yes, the carriage mishap did delay me a bit. Nevertheless, I'm here now. Did I miss much?"

"Not much unless you find it interesting to see a hundred men asking the same question all over town."

Petra laughed softly and blushed. There was a moment of silence that passed between them and then Petra saw her Godfather. "Oh, Godfather!" she called to him. They approached, exchanged greetings, introductions, and chatted casually for a few minutes. Appropriately and reluctantly, Sir Manfred excused himself after a few minutes so that Petra and her Godfather could continue in private.

"Godfather, did you find us a place to stay for tonight?" Petra asked while looking after Sir Manfred.

"Not yet. I gather from your inquiry that you haven't found a place either. I don't know what we should do. It's getting late—how goes the quest?"

"Not well…" Petra's voice trailed off. She had noticed a

well-dressed couple stopping to talk to Sir Manfred. She watched as he spoke a few words to them and then she saw them look in her direction. The couple approached Petra. She could see Sir Manfred smile broadly and wave to her. She waved back as the couple approached.

"Excuse us, Mistress. I'm Doctor Schnellretter and this is my wife and assistant, Anna." They shook hands, curtsied, and bowed while Petra introduced herself and her Godfather.

The doctor continued, "The gentleman told us that this carriage was not his, but belongs to you, Mistress."

Petra nodded in agreement.

"We're passing through Dillsburg on a medical mission to Rellischwald. We stopped briefly to rest and our carriage was stolen."

"Luckily our medical supplies were not in the carriage at the time," the doctor's wife, Anna added.

"Yes," he confirmed, "but nonetheless, we are without transportation.

We were hoping that you could lease us your carriage, and we
would return it to you by tomorrow evening, or
at the very latest, two days. We do have the
resources to compensate you and we can
offer you some excellent references.
We're desperate. There are lives at
stake. We must deliver medicines to
Rellischwald—they are suffering
from a terrible outbreak of influenza and pneumonia."

Petra looked at their pleading faces and remembered how
she had needed help just the day before. *"How can I refuse
them?"* she reprimanded herself, *"I may be on a quest, but they
are in serious need...to help people who are suffering."* She
looked to her Godfather. Her mind raced. She could see that
they were waiting for a reply. Finally, after weighing everything
in her mind, she was inspired. "I cannot be without my
transportation for such a long period. However, we may be able
to find a compromise. Do you know someone in Rellischwald
from whom you could obtain return transportation?"

"Yes, I do. What are you proposing, Mistress?"

"Do you know if they might have accommodations for
my Godfather and I to stay for the night?"

"Yes, I'm sure they do. Are you headed toward Rellischwald?"

"Well, I could be. There doesn't seem to be a room available here in Dillsburg for the night. I will need my transportation tomorrow, but if we travel together to Rellischwald..."

"Oh, Mistress! That would be wonderful!" Anna exclaimed.

"It might be the solution we need." Doctor Schnellretter scratched his beard while deep in thought, "If we changed our route a bit...yes, that might work."

"Sweetheart, you're talking to yourself again," Anna teased.

"Yes, I was just thinking. If we change our route, we'll only need to make one stop on our way to Master Schnitzelmeier's house. We could all stay there and Anna and I could use one of their carriages to make our other visits and deliveries, leaving you free to continue on your journey in the morning."

"Perfect. Bring your things and we'll be on our way. The hour does grow late."

"Thank you, thank you, Mistress. Your kindness knows no bounds. We have these bags and I'll retrieve the others." Doctor

Schnellretter handed the bags to Petra's Godfather and turned to his wife, "Anna, stay here. I will return momentarily and we will finally be on our way." He kissed her on the cheek and rushed off.

Doctor Schnellretter did indeed rush back and they were on the road into the forests of Rellischwald in less than half-an-hour.

The road through the forest was easy and quiet. Petra rather enjoyed the quiet of the forest to the noise and commotion she encountered in Dillsburg. She also enjoyed the pleasant company and conversation of Doctor Schnellretter and Anna.

They were a very charming couple: intelligent and refined. At times, they were comfortably quiet and Petra stared peacefully out her carriage window. The scenery of the forest was soothing, but it did get increasingly colder. They all pulled their cloaks on a little tighter and then pulled out blankets to cover themselves for more warmth.

In the afternoon mist that covered the forest floor, Petra noticed several families of rabbits nibbling and playing along the roadside. Against the darkening sky, she even saw a couple of stags standing guard as they passed.

It was cold and the wind carried with it the promise of snow. Hours passed as they traveled and in the darkness of late twilight, they made their first stop at a lumber mill and the home of Master Holzfaeller.

Dr. Schnellretter and Anna quickly climbed out of the carriage. They introduced Petra and her Godfather, but then asked to be taken immediately to Master Holzfaeller's littlest daughter who had pneumonia.

Petra's Godfather tended to their horses and the carriage, while Petra talked with Master Holzfaeller's oldest son, Karl.

"Mistress, what brings you to the forests of Rellischwald? Do you have relatives up here?"

"No. I've never been here before. I'm on a mission or quest of sorts, and I've been somewhat detoured. I find the area quite enchanting and your home is exquisite. I've never seen such beautiful woodwork!"

"Most of us up here work in the lumber mills—especially since the ore mines closed.

Our family has been in the lumber business for several generations, but many of the residents up here used to be miners. Work is scarce right now—but I shouldn't bother you, Mistress. I'm sorry…with my sister's illness and well, I'm sorry."

"No apologies are necessary. I'm sincerely interested. As I told you, I'm on a quest—I don't get the opportunity to travel that often, so I'm enjoying every minute of it. Do you and your family have many problems with animals up here? I've heard mention of problems with deer, wolves, and even bears."

"Oh Mistress. We've lived up here a long time. We have certain tricks we use to keep the animals away from the house, out of our berry patches, and from eating our nuts and mushrooms."

"Tricks?"

"Well…for instance, to keep the bears away, we'll fell a tree where a large, male bear has made his markings. We'll take the felled tree and some of the earth surrounding the tree and prop it up in an area where we want to ward off bears—we'll spread some of the earth around there as well."

"And that works?"

" No bear will enter the territory of another larger male bear."

"And the wolves and deer?"

"It pretty much wards off the wolves too. As for the deer, we just construct some heavy-duty fencing and provide feeding areas for them outside our gardens. "

"That's really fascinating. I wish I were heading back to Heinzinger. They could benefit from the information. They're constantly battling animals coming in and destroying their crops and livestock."

Karl took Petra around the house and showed her some of their hand-made furniture, and at her request, he took her outside to see the lumber mill itself. They were just returning, when they were met at the front door by Master Holzfaeller, his wife, and Dr. Schnellretter and Anna.

"Thank you so much, Doctor," Master Holzfaeller said sincerely while shaking Dr. Schnellretter's hand. "You don't know how much we appreciate your attention and care. We've been so worried."

"Don't mention it. Just make sure she takes the medicine I left her. Also make sure that she gets ample bed rest and drinks plenty of fluids."

"Karl! Why have you taken the young Mistress out into the cold? She should be warming up inside. Did you offer her something warm to drink? What are you doing out here?" scolded Master Holzfaeller.

Before Karl could reply, Petra boldly spoke up, "Oh, Master Holzfaeller, Karl has been so kind and hospitable. He even came out here at my request to show me your wonderful accomplishments here at the lumber mill. I've learned so much! I hope you don't mind that I asked him to show me around."

"Of course not, Mistress. I was just worried that you had been ill-treated. I'm glad to hear that you enjoyed yourself. Do you wish to come in and have a warm drink?"

"No, no thank you."

"Actually, it is getting very late and we still must make it up to Master Schnitzelmeier's place," Dr. Schnellretter interjected.

"Yes, yes it is late and it looks as though we may be getting some snow tonight. My, it is cold. Thank you again for coming. Are you sure there isn't anything we could do for you or anything you need to take with you?" Master Holzfaeller asked.

"No, no thank..."

"Well, there is one thing," Petra interrupted.

"What do you need, Mistress?"

"As I have told your son, I am on a quest. Do any of you know of an artist who makes Christmas ornaments entirely of glass?"

Dr. Schnellretter and Anna looked at each other; their eyes wide and their mouths open in surprise. Master Holzfaeller shook his head and looked to his wife and son.

"No, Mistress. We have not heard of anyone up here."

"Petra!" Anna exclaimed. "You didn't tell us that you are on the King's quest!"

"I thought you knew."

"Petra, I know the ornament maker! He lives back home near us in Klaussendorf."

Petra blinked several times. "In Klaussendorf? Are you sure?" she uttered in disbelief.

"Yes, I'm sure. He's my cousin, Gustav Baumschmuecker. Why didn't you tell us? Why didn't you ask?"

"I don't know. I was so taken with your plight that I completely forgot to ask."

"Well," Dr. Schnellretter interrupted, "we had better get on our way. It's starting to snow."

They said their "Goodbye's" and wished them all a Merry Christmas and a healthy New Year, and they were on their way once again.

Petra was excited. She half-listened as Anna explained about her cousin, where he lives, what kind of ornaments he makes, and how she'll give her exact instructions on how to get there. Petra was busy thinking.

"Did they tell anyone else in Dillsburg? Surely, someone would have asked them. Was that why Sir Manfred smiled as he did?" She couldn't ask them, it wouldn't be right.

"If they did tell them, then what. Those contestants would be on their way to Klaussendorf and I'm in Rellischwald—

*on the other side of the Kingdom.
What luck...now I know where to
find the ornament maker... and...I'm
heading the wrong way!"*

Petra continued to suffer in
silence. It started snowing and it wasn't
quite as cold as before.

As the forest grew black with the
darkness of night, Petra noticed some lights
twinkling between snowflakes in the distance. Dr. Schnellretter
remarked, "That's where we're headed. We should be there
soon, and none too late. It looks as though we may get a
blizzard tonight."

"Great...a blizzard. What else can happen?" Petra
complained inwardly. Outwardly, she nodded with mild interest.

Chapter Five

pproximately another twenty minutes passed until their carriage pulled up to a wonderful mountain chalet. The Schnitzelmeier's greeted them warmly. Two young sons promptly took their horses and their carriage into a large barn, while their guests made their way inside to warm themselves in front of a huge fireplace.

Petra looked around. The chalet was magnificent. The woodwork was intricate—delicate in some places—yet solid. Huge beams stretched across the roof and the ceiling pitched high—

so high that the rafters hid in the darkness of shadows against the firelight.

The Schnitzelmeier's had decorated the main room for Christmas. Of course the Christmas tree was not up yet, (that didn't go up until Christmas Eve), but the mantle and tables were hung with pine garland and the tables were laden with cookies and bowls of nuts and fruit.

Petra wandered admiringly, when suddenly she noticed something else: beautiful wood-carved figures adorned each table. One carving was a soldier baring a row of white teeth. Another was an old man smoking a pipe— and there was smoke coming out of his mouth!"

"What's this? It's wonderful!" Petra squealed with delight.

"Oh, that's an incense smoker man. My son-in-law made it," explained Master Schnitzelmeier's wife, Eva. "You open it here," she took it apart at the midsection, "and you place a small piece of lit incense inside," she put it back together, "and it smokes out of its mouth."

59

"It's wonderful! Look!" Petra called out to the others. "Isn't it grand?"

"Let me show you mine," Eva's youngest daughter, Emily, cried out. "Look you put a nut in his mouth, push down the handle, and you can crack nuts!"

Emily placed a nut between the soldier's small rows of wooden teeth.

CR-R-AAACK!

"See! Isn't he wonderful? I received him for Nikolaus Day." Emily cradled the wooden soldier in her arms.

"It certainly is fine. May I see him?" Petra asked.

"Sure."

"My, he is handsome, almost like a Prince, wouldn't you say?"

"Yes, I think he is a Prince," Emily agreed.

"Did you see that over there?"

asked Alfred, Emily's younger brother. "Did you see the whirligig thingy over there? It's my favorite."

"It's called a Christmas Pyramid," Emily corrected him while she rolled her eyes.

Alfred ignored her, took Petra's hand, and led her and the other guests over to another table in a corner of the room. On the table, stood a large multilevel wood house with intricately carved figures, animals, and trees— depicting the nativity. "See, it's the baby Jesus, Mary, and Joseph. There are the three wise men and here are the shepherds and their sheep."

Emily chimed in, "Inside the top window are the angels. I like the angels."

Alfred narrowed his eyes as he looked at Emily, he continued, "See, there's a fan at the very top. And...and the candles... Mama?" He looked around, "Mama, can you light

the candles so that she can see how it works? Pleeeeeease?"

"Just a minute," Eva soothed.

Eva came over and lit four candles that stood at the base of the nativity house. As she lit the candles, the fan above the house began to turn. As it turned, the tiny scenes spun, creating miniature vignettes at different levels within the house.

"How wonderful!" Petra cheered.

"My Papa made it," Alfred stated proudly.

"I've never seen anything like it. It's absolutely wonderful. What did you call it?" Petra asked Emily.

"A Christmas Pyramid."

"A Christmas Pyramid. I've truly never seen anything like it. Have you, Anna?"

"No. It's beautiful. Oh, I just love it! How does it work?"

"By the heat of the candles," answered Master Schnitzelmeier, "the heat rises and turns the blades of the fan, which turns the scenes at each level."

"It really is fantastic. So is the nutcracker and…what was it? A smoker? You know these would make wonderful gifts."

"Gifts?" Anna laughed. "I want one!"

"Do you sell them?" Dr. Schnellretter asked.

"We've been thinking about it," explained Master Schnitzelmeier. "Work has been scarce and many of us up here used to work in the mines. My son-in-law and his brothers are all out of work. They've begun working in the lumberyard, but as I said, work is scarce. We started making these as gifts this Christmas, but we were thinking of taking some of them to the other villages. We weren't sure if they would sell."

"Well, I know you've made one sale already," Dr. Schnellretter said as he looked at his wife. "I don't think we'll be leaving here without one of your pyramids. And if I leave it to my wife, we'll be buying a nutcracker and smoker as well."

"Me too!" Petra added.

"We don't have many made yet, but I'm sure we'll have enough for you all. However, you won't be able to buy them from me. You must take them along as gifts."

"Oh no, Master Schnitzelmeier. That would be too much to ask!" Dr. Schnellretter complained.

"Nonsense! After all, you've made a special journey here to help our community in a time of need. For that, I can only offer these crafts as a small token of our gratitude."

Everyone objected, but Master Schnitzelmeier wouldn't hear it and stood his ground. After some additional pleasantries, Dr. Schnellretter and Anna went with Master Schnitzelmeier to visit a few neighbors and his eldest son-in-law, all who were suffering from pneumonia. Petra and her Godfather went to their rooms to rest a bit and freshen up. Petra took the extra time before a late dinner to write in her journal. Much had happened that day and she didn't want to forget anything. She was just about finished when she heard voices down the hall and the smell of dinner that beckoned her—it was late and she was famished.

Dinner was as warm and hearty as the company. Eva cooked a wonderful meal. Petra especially liked the mushroom medley and gravy.

"These mushrooms are like none other I've ever eaten. There seem to be several kinds of mushrooms here and they taste almost like meat."

"Thank you. Mushrooms are a specialty around here—mushroom, nuts, and berries. You learn to make do with what you have," Eva replied.

"Make do? These are delicious."

"You might be interested to know," said Dr. Schnellretter, "they grow nearly twelve different kinds of mushrooms and more than 20 different berries. Some are edible, but some are poisonous and can only be used for medicinal purposes."

"Really? Do you use mushrooms and berries in your medicines?" Petra asked.

"Yes, in some. In fact, we often collect specimens and take them back to our apothecary in Klaussendorf."

Eva and one of her older daughters cleared the table to make room for dessert. She brought out hot peppermint tea and a huge torte for her guests to enjoy.

Petra tasted her first forkful and her eyes rolled back in approval, "MMMMMmmmm! This is good. I've never had crust like this, and the filling...Is it berry preserves?"

"It is. As I told you, we don't get much in the way of wheat and grain up here. The crust is made of ground hazelnuts, sugar, cinnamon, and butter. The filling is a mixed berry preserve."

"It's delicious, well…I guess you can tell, because it's gone," Petra laughed.

"Do you want another slice?"

"Yes, I do…but I better not…I'm so full I can hardly breathe. I couldn't eat another bite."

Petra lingered a bit longer, sipping her peppermint tea, and enjoying the conversation. The hour grew late and soon they excused themselves one-by-one and went to their separate rooms.

Petra wrote a few additional notes in her journal before going to bed. Even though she had a long day and she was incredibly tired, Petra found it difficult to fall asleep. She kept thinking about the other contestants and whether or not they were already on their way to Klaussendorf. Finally, she convinced herself that there was nothing she could possibly do, and with that thought, she finally fell asleep.

Chapter Six

The morning came and it was dark and gray. It had snowed all night and a light snow was still falling when Petra opened her eyes and looked out the window. It was later than usual when Petra arose from her bed. She dressed and as she came down the hall, her Godfather met her.

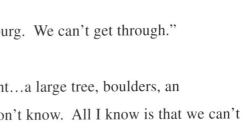

"Bad news, Petra."

"What?"

"The road is blocked."

"Which road?"

"The road to Dillsburg. We can't get through."

"Why?"

"The snow last night…a large tree, boulders, an avalanche…something, I don't know. All I know is that we can't get through."

"How long?"

"A few days."

"Oh, no…" Petra started to panic. She could feel her throat tightening. She fought back tears and cleared her throat. "There must be another way out of here." Petra saw Master Schnitzelmeier and called out to  him, "Excuse me! Master Schnitzelmeier? My Godfather just told me that the road to Dillsburg is closed—blocked. I must get to Klaussendorf today. Is there another way to get to Dillsburg?"

"Do you need to get to Dillsburg or to Klaussendorf?"

 "Klaussendorf."

"Well, you can get to Klaussendorf by way of Breinland instead of through Dillsburg."

"Is the road to Breinland open?"

"Yes, but its a mountain pass and you won't be able to traverse it using your carriage.  You'll need a sleigh. I have one you can use. I'll have my sons prepare it for you."

"Thank you. The carriage I am using though, belongs to the wheelwright in Gurkenheim."

"I'll make sure it gets to him."

"And I'll make sure your sleigh is returned to you."

Petra and her Godfather had a light breakfast and hastily packed their things onto the sleigh. Master Schnitzelmeier gave them some additional supplies; blankets, warm hats, scarves, and gloves; directions and advice as to where to stop in Breinland. In addition, he also loaded them up with the gifts he promised them the night before. Eva gave Petra a large jar of her berry preserves and Anna gave Petra a letter of introduction and complete instructions on how to find her cousin in Klaussendorf. Petra was overwhelmed. She hugged them all and promised to see them again. Petra's Godfather slapped the reins and the sleigh took off. Petra was teary-eyed as she waved and wished them all a Merry Christmas.

Riding in the sleigh was quite different from the carriage.

The sleigh glided smoothly over the landscape. It was a little colder, but Petra nestled under the blankets and covered her

nose and ears with a scarf. She could see so much more than she could from the carriage. She loved looking up at the sky.

They slid through the mountain pass and the forests of Rellischwald for hours. The light snow became thicker: the flakes clustered together and looked like large white feathers floating down from the billowing gray clouds. Petra wondered if

her Godfather was warm enough. She asked a few times, and he always said he was fine, but still she worried.

The day seemed to be getting darker, and yet Petra knew it couldn't be much later than noon. *"The sun should be high in the sky,"* Petra mumbled as she looked up through the falling flakes of snow. "How much longer do you think it will be until we get to Breinland? Shouldn't we almost be there?" she called out to her Godfather.

"I figure it might be another hour. The wind and snow are starting to slow us down."

Petra settled back under her blankets and watched the feathery flakes fall. It wasn't long before she fell asleep.

A little more than an hour had passed when Petra heard her Godfather, "Petra, wake up. We're stopping here in Breinland."

Petra cleared her mind as she slowly awoke from her pleasant dreams. There was an ample amount of snow covering her blanket and she noticed her toes were a little numb. She looked around. They had stopped the sleigh beneath an eave of a solid looking house—the stonework of the house was impressive. She looked out from underneath the eaves and saw nothing but white. "I'm sorry, Godfather. What did you say?"

"We're stopping here. The wind and snow are too much. The horses need rest and warmth and so do we. Come on."

"It does look bad. How late is it? Where are we?"

"It's early afternoon. We're in the heart of Breinland at a place that Master Schnitzelmeier suggested. We should have made it here before lunch. I'm sorry, but if the snow and wind don't let up, we may have to spend the night here and attempt to get to Klaussendorf tomorrow."

"Tomorrow?" Petra climbed out of the sleigh in a panic. "Tomorrow will be day four! I'll have only one day to get the ornament and make it back to the palace."

"I know, but there's nothing we can do. Besides, I'm sure all the competitors are in the same predicament. You can't travel in this weather. Now, don't panic and let's go inside."

Reluctantly, Petra followed her Godfather inside. It was warm and there was a huge fire blazing in the fireplace.

"Welcome! Welcome! Come in and warm yourselves," a ruddy-faced man cheerily greeted them. "I hear you've come from my good friend's house, Master Schnitzelmeier. Welcome, have a seat. Would you like something warm to drink?" Before either of them could answer, the gentleman turned to a young lady, "Louisa, get them a couple of hot ciders. They need to thaw out." He turned back to Petra, "I'm Master Steinhauer, but my friends call me Hans."

"I'm Petra and this is Arthur, my Godfather," Petra offered in the spirit of informality.

"It's a pleasure. We'll have your things brought in shortly, and my boys will look after your horses and sleigh. We weren't expecting company, but you are certainly welcome. We'll do our best to accommodate you. Is there anything that you might need?"

"Well, we hadn't thought of staying. Do you know if the snow storm should be letting up soon?"

"I don't think so. If it does, it will be nearly dark. Where are you headed?"

"Klaussendorf. I had hoped to make it there by nightfall."

"Not in this weather. Perhaps, if the storm  lets up by this evening, you can get an early start in the morning. With good weather, you can make it there by afternoon. Stay the night, eat, and rest; Klaussendorf will be there in the morning," Hans said with a broad happy smile.

Petra managed a weak smile. She couldn't help feeling depressed and thought, *"...yet, another set back."* Hans showed them to their rooms and she lay across her bed for the rest of the afternoon, occasionally staring out the window, wishing the snow to stop falling. While she lay there, she did notice the wonderful stonework that made up the walls of her room. Her room also had a fireplace with a huge stone mantle and bench. She noticed the floor was also made of stone and as the firelight flickered, the floor sparkled as though the stone imprisoned flecks of gold and silver.

It was getting dark outside and Petra realized that she had spent the entire afternoon moping and daydreaming. She hoped their host thought she was sleeping and wouldn't notice her poor disposition. She decided to freshen up and join them. To her surprise and delight, they were a lively bunch—just what she needed to lift her spirits.

"Petra!" Hans called out, "Come join us. Come meet my family. You're just in time for dinner. Come sit here," he pulled out a chair for Petra next to him. A young maiden came in and placed a large bowl on the table. "This is one of my daughters: Louisa."

Hans went around the table introducing his family—his wife: Lina, sons: Otto and Max, daughters: Louisa, Elsie, and Hedi, son-in-laws: Andreas, Karli, and Heinrich, daughter in-law (Otto's wife): Helena, and Otto and Helena's newborn child: Johann.

Hans presented his family with great pride, "My wife's side of the family and my daughters' husbands are all shepherds: goats and sheep. They produce the finest wool and tastiest goat cheese in the entire Kingdom; however, my side of the family and my sons are all stonemasons. We build solid walls, warm hearths, and sturdy fences."

"I noticed your beautiful floors. Did you make these floors?" Petra asked.

"My father and I installed them. We built the entire house when I was a young man. My father and mother have since passed away, but a little of them remains here in the house. Stone is virtually everlasting. Each stone can tell a story—and when I pass, I hope to leave my mark behind in a few of the stones so that my grandchildren will remember their grandfather and their great grandparents, as well."

"Oh, look. He's going to get all teary-eyed about his rocks again," his son-in-law, Karli, teased.

"I suppose you would rather have him tell a story of the great tradition of goat herding," Otto teased back.

"Well, you wouldn't see me getting all weepy about it."

"Oh, how about when you tell the story about your favorite ewe—last spring?" Otto prodded with a smile.

Everyone at the table seemed to be suppressing a giggle.

"As I remember it," Otto continued, "you were practically bawling like a baby when she finally gave birth to those twins."

"She had a hard time…" Karli whined in defense, "and…"

Before Karli could finish his sentence, he was drowned out with laughter. He had no choice but to give up and start laughing at himself.

Hans wiped a happy tear of laughter from his eyes, raised his glass, and toasted, "A solid house, hearty food, and warm clothing—we're a blessed family!" he laughed heartily.

Petra loved the friendly banter that continued all through dinner. The dinner was a filling meal of lentil and potato stew, flatbread, and goat cheese. Petra had never tasted goat cheese. She found the taste a new favorite. The conversation was warm and friendly. For dessert, Hans's wife served a warm rice pudding with fruit compote and hot cider.

Petra's cheeks were rosy and bright. Hans's family was delightful—and funny. She hadn't laughed so hard since she was a child and she found herself wishing that she had brothers. After dinner, they moved to sit in front of the fire and drink their ciders.

"Looks like it's stopped snowing and the stars are coming out. It should be excellent traveling weather in the morning," Hans announced as he looked out the front door.

"Petra, so that you don't get a chill, take this and wrap yourself in it," Hans's wife, Lina, offered Petra a beautifully crocheted wool wrap. "I made it myself from a blend of wool from our mountain sheep and goats' wool. I want you to have it. Please take it with you as a gift from me. It will keep you warm and it repels moisture."

"It's beautiful! What a wonderful gift. Oh, it feels soooo soft," cooed Petra as she snuggled down into the shawl. "Thank you so much for everything. Our stay here really has been delightful." Petra beamed as she sipped her hot cider. "I was feeling a bit down about being delayed, but being with your family has really brightened my spirits."

"We're all delighted to have you here," Hans replied.

"Your home is so warm and cozy, and the stone work is marvelous. I'm particularly impressed with the tile work on the stove, benches, and your floors. Do you do cobblestone too?"

"Cobblestone? Of course! Why?"

"They could use your talents down in Gurkenheim. Their roads are in bad repair and they don't seem to have a decent mason."

"Gurkenheim? Well, we've done a little work in Dillsburg, but we've never gone that far south. We'll have to look in to it."

"You should take some of that delicious goat cheese as well. I've never tasted anything like it. They have a bakery in Gurkenheim...with their bread and your cheese..." Petra sighed deeply.

Hans smiled proudly, "I'm glad you enjoyed it. Now, I think it's getting late, and if you want to make an early start in the morning, you best get your rest."

Petra stretched and yawned comfortably, "I guess you're right. I sure did have a good time tonight. Thank you."

Petra said goodnight to her Godfather giving him a kiss. She gave Hans a little kiss on the cheek, and she gave Lina a big hug and thanked her again for the beautiful shawl before making her way back to her room.

Once again she wrote in her journal, laid out her things for the next day, and with warm thoughts and rosy cheeks, she fell asleep.

Chapter Seven

*I*t was still dark outside when a knock at the door awakened Petra. Her Godfather whispered loudly, "Petra! Time to get up. We want to leave early. 'Remember?"

"Yes, I remember. I'm up. I'm up."

Petra dressed quickly, ate a hot breakfast, and reluctantly left the warm and friendly company of the Steinhauer family. On the road under a clear sky, Petra trembled with thoughts of excitement. Finally, she would make it to Klaussendorf and find the ornament maker. They would have to rush to make it back to the palace. She hoped and prayed that there wouldn't be any more snowstorms. She looked at the slowly brightening sky—it was clear. *"Not a cloud in the sky,"* she mused happily.

The roads were smooth as glass and they glided easily along the mountain pass. They didn't have time to stop for lunch. Lina had packed them each a lunch of goat cheese sandwiches and some hot cider, so they ate on the road. During the long ride, Petra found herself dozing off—she really hated getting up so early and the ride made her sleepy. Occasionally Petra awoke, watched the scenery pass by, gauged the time by the position of the sun in the sky, and dozed off again.

It was late afternoon, when Petra noticed that they were out of the mountains and entering a quaint little village. Rolling hills of fruit orchards surrounded the tiny village of Klaussendorf. The heavy snow burdened the trees and icicles of varying length clung to the branches, glistening in the slowly setting sun.

"What a beautiful village," Petra thought admiringly. Then she called to her Godfather, "There it is, Godfather! Just think, all these days of searching, and the ornament maker lives right down there in that tiny little village."

Petra's Godfather looked back at her briefly and smiled, "It's been quite an adventure, hasn't it?"

"Yes! We're so close now that I can hardly wait."

"We'll be there within an hour. Settle back and try to relax—if you can."

Petra tried to calm herself, but her heart kept pounding. She watched as they passed orchard after orchard. "What kind of trees are those? Do you know?" she shouted.

"I think they are apple trees, maybe some pear. It's hard to tell this time of year."

"Oh." Petra settled back again. She was so nervous that she found herself playing with the buttons on her cloak. She twisted and twisted, fiddled and turned. Before she knew it, one

of the buttons was loose in her hand. *"Oh, great, that was bright!"* she admonished herself. She looked to see from where she had loosened the button. She quickly found that it came from her sleeve: a decorative button meant only for adornment. *"Well at least I really don't need it,"* she half-muttered. She tucked the button in her pocket just as they were sledding into the village.

Petra looked with great interest as they passed each building and every street. She had given the directions to her Godfather and he seemed to know exactly where he was going.

Suddenly, they turned down a long winding street, lined with trees and lovely little homes. They slowed and halted in front of a particularly charming little house.

"This should be it, Petra," her Godfather said.

The house was set back from the road and there was pathway leading up to the door. In front of the house, Petra could see a small child playing in the snow. She flung off the blankets and practically leapt out of the sleigh without her Godfather's help. *"Where's my letter?"* she said to herself while patting down her pockets. *"Oh, here…"* she said while taking a deep breath. "Wish me luck."

"Good Luck, sweetheart. I'll see where to take our sleigh while you go in. I'll see you later."

Petra made her way carefully up the path, taking care not to slip on the icy pathway. As she approached, she could see that the small child in front of the house was a little girl, and she was building a snowman. As Petra came closer, she noticed that the little girl was crying.

"Hello, little girl. What's the matter? Why are you crying?"

"My snowman..."

"He's a fine looking snowman. Did you build him yourself?"

"Yes, but he's not finished," she sniffled and wiped her eyes with a mitten.

"Not finished? I think you've done a wonderful job!"

"He's not finished—he doesn't have a nose!" she sobbed. "My mother won't let me have a carrot and I've looked everywhere for something to use, but I can't find anything!"

"Hmmmmm...maybe I can help. First, let me introduce myself. My name is Petra. Now, what's your name?"

Still sniffling she replied, "Kristina. This is my house."

"Well, Kristina...we need a nose for this handsome

looking snowman. You know, if he doesn't have a nose, that means he'll never have to catch it when it runs…his mother will never have to blow his nose…AND…he'll never sneeze!"

Kristina giggled and laughed, "But he'll never be able to smell things like Mama's apple strudel."

"Ah yes, that would be a problem. Wait, I have it!" Petra reached into her pocket and pulled out the button that had loosened from her cloak. She handed it to Kristina, "Will this work?"

Kristina's eyes widened. The button was big, round and covered with crimson velvet. "It's perfect!" she squealed. She placed the button on the snowman's face. "Look, his nose is red—he must be cold!" she laughed. "Oh, thank you! Thank you!" she hugged Petra.

"You're welcome. I'm glad I could help. Are you all right now? No more tears?"

"No more tears. I'm fine…" she turned to admire her snowman and then asked, "Are you here to see my Papa?"

"Well, if your Papa is Master Baumschmuecker, then yes."

"I thought so. He's had many visitors in the past few days. He's in the workshop at the side of the house. I'll show you."

Kristina took Petra's hand and led her to a side entrance. They went up a few stairs and through a door at the top of the landing. The door creaked as they entered. "That's my Papa over there talking to that lady," Kristina whispered. "I told you he's been busy. Just wait here. He'll see you."

"Thank you," Petra whispered back.

Kristina took off her mittens and cloak and sat down in a corner behind a desk. Petra took off her gloves and looked around. It was an odd looking workshop. Actually, it was a mess. There were tables, shelves, and a desk. There were papers and boxes strewn all over the place. She could barely take a step—there was debris everywhere.

As she looked around, she began to overhear the conversation between Master Baumschmuecker and the other rather stately looking woman. Petra heard Master Baumschmuecker saying, "...It's a new technique. Each ornament is mouth–blown out of glass, lined with sterling silver..."

"Lined with sterling silver! Goodness, how do you do that?" the lady inquired.

"I use a process similar to that of making mirrors. I inject silver nitrate, ammonia, and sugar into the glass ornament. Then I dip the ornament into hot water to facilitate a chemical reaction..."

"Oh my, that sounds dangerous!"

"No, no, it's simple chemistry. You see, the hot water and the ammonia causes the silver to release from the silver nitrate and the sugar adheres the silver to the glass—on the inside of the ornament. Then the ornament looks like a shiny mirror."

"Really?"

"After the ornament is silvered, it must go through several layers of painting. Each ornament is hand-painted and hand-glittered. In between each process, the ornament must dry. It's at least a seven-day process for each piece."

"Seven days?"

"Seven days at a minimum. If you want special pieces made, then I must first create a sculpture, a casting, and a mold. That process can take a month or more."

"A month?"

"So you see, tomorrow is Christmas Eve and I simply cannot have the pieces you requested by tomorrow. It's just not possible. Besides, I don't have any materials or supplies left. I must wait until my shipments arrive next month to begin making them again."

"Well, yes. That's a shame, but I do understand…I was just hoping," her voice trailed off. "They are just so divine…I must have them for next Christmas, then. Can you begin on my order after the holidays? I will certainly make it worth your while."

"Yes, of course. Make a list of what you want and we'll discuss it in detail after the holidays. Until then, I wish you and your family a Merry Christmas."

"Thank you very much, Master Baumschmuecker. Merry Christmas to you and yours, as well. I'll see you after the holidays. Good day." The lady left smiling and bowed slightly as she passed Petra. Master Baumschmuecker noticed Petra and turned his attention to her.

"Yes, Mistress. Please excuse the mess. There's been a…how can I put it…a sudden interest in my work and I'm still trying to recover. How may I help you?"

"I am Mistress Petra. I recently had the pleasure of traveling with your cousin Anna and her husband, Doctor Schnellretter. I bear a letter of introduction…" Petra handed him the letter. For some reason she had a sickly feeling in her stomach and her mouth felt so dry she could barely speak.

"Oh, a friend of the family," he smiled, "for a moment there, I thought you might be here about my glass ornaments. It's been crazy around here." He broke the seal of the letter and continued chatting as he unfolded it. "Yesterday was the worst. Our royal highnesses decided to hold a contest of some sort and made my ornaments the objects of a quest. I was completely deluged...they took...every..." he slowed as he read the letter, "piece...Oh dear! I'm so sorry!"

Petra couldn't speak. She bit her lip to fight back her tears.

Master Baumschmuecker continued apologetically, "I'm so very sorry. I didn't know you were on the same royal quest."

Petra felt light-headed. She heard a rushing in her ears. Somehow, she summoned her strength to ask, "You don't have a single ornament?" Her lip quivered and her hands shook as she tried to stay calm.

"Not one, I'm so sorry. Look, they practically tore this place apart. Even the few pieces we had for our own tree are gone. They took everything."

Petra couldn't hold back. The words just burst out, "No! I've come all this way! I only need one—just one! There must be one left. I can't return to the palace empty handed." Tears were streaming down her cheeks, and her cheeks burned red with the shame of her outburst.

Master Baumschmuecker didn't have the words to console her. He felt a little uncomfortable and began shifting

boxes and looking under papers in a haphazard effort to look for a single remaining ornament that he knew did not exist.

Master Baumschmuecker was at a loss, he whispered to his daughter, "Stay here, I'll go get Mama."

With a worried and compassionate look, Kristina nodded her head. Master Baumschmuecker hurried out the door.

Petra was beyond consolation. She let herself collapse to her knees in grief. Through tear-filled eyes, she aimlessly searched through the debris-strewn floor of the little workshop. "There must be just one…" she sobbed.

Kristina couldn't bear to see her new friend in such pain. She knelt down beside her and patted her shoulder sympathetically, "Please, don't cry."

Petra looked at Kristina. *"How can she possibly understand? She doesn't know…"* Petra thought as she looked at her little friend.

Kristina must have seen it in her eyes, because she looked down in shame. Then she crawled under a desk at the back of the little workshop.

"Nice. Now, I've scared a little girl. Am I really that selfish?" Petra thought shaking her head. "I'm sorry Kristina! I didn't mean for you to go away," Petra called through tears.

"I'm getting something!" she called out from under the desk.

Kristina came back with a little wooden box and sat cross-legged next to Petra. Petra did the same and took a handkerchief from her sleeve to wipe her eyes. "What's that?"

"It's my special stuff." Kristina opened the box, pulled out something shiny, and handed it to Petra. "Will this work?"

Petra took the object from Kristina's little hand. She stared at it in disbelief. "It's an ornament! A glass ornament! Oh, Kristina!" Petra held the little ornament up to admire it. It was small, very shiny, and green.

"It's a...?" Petra wondered.

"It's a pickle!" Kristina answered. "My Mama and Papa call me their little pickle, because my Mama ate so many pickles when I was in her tummy. My Papa made me this ornament and I saved it in my box of special stuff. So, will it work?"

"This is a very special ornament. I can't take this from you."

"But I want you to have it! You gave me a nose for my snowman. I want to give you my pickle ornament! Pleeeeease take it. I heard that the King and Queen are planning to hang all the ornaments from the contest on the Christmas tree at the palace. I would love to know that my pickle is there. Pleeeease take it."

Petra cried tears of joy and wrapped her arms around Kristina. "Oh, thank you! Thank you! I'll make sure your pickle is on the tree," Petra promised.

"Are you all right now? No more tears?" Kristina asked.

"No more tears," Petra laughed.

Petra and Kristina were getting up from the floor when they realized that Master Baumschmuecker and his wife were standing in the room. Petra straightened her clothes, hair, and dabbed her swollen eyes with her handkerchief.

"I'm sorry, I didn't hear you come in." She cleared her throat and tried to compose herself. "Your daughter is truly heaven-sent. She is such a special child—an angel. She gave me this to take back with me for the contest." Petra showed them the pickle ornament.

"And guess what? My pickle is going to be on the King and Queen's Christmas tree in the palace. I told her that's what I wanted and she promised me. Isn't that wonderful? My pickle will be in the palace!"

"Yes, Kristina. We heard. That's so wonderful!" Kristina's mother said as she hugged her daughter. Still smiling a proud smile, she said to Petra, "I'm Marianne, Kristina's mother. It's a pleasure to meet you."

"The pleasure is all mine. I am Petra, daughter of Sir Nicholas and Lady Karolina," she stated while curtseying.

"Well, tragedy averted!" Master Baumschmuecker interjected. "Why don't you come over into the house? We have accommodations for you and your coachman. I would love to hear more about your royal quest and we can get to know each other over dinner."

"You are very kind. I'm so sorry that I became so emotional. It's been a long week. You're very kind."

"Not at all, not at all…come now…follow us. You can freshen up and rest before dinner."

Petra followed Master Baumschmuecker and Lady

Marianne out of the workshop and into the charming little house she had seen from the road. Kristina held her hand the whole way and led her to a guest room where she could rest. Petra's Godfather had unloaded the sleigh and Petra's things were already in the room.

Petra was exhausted and emotionally drained. She changed her clothes and tried to sit down and write in her journal, but the words just didn't seem to flow. She caressed the edges of the little box in front of her. It was the box in which she always carried her best quill pens and her favorite inks. It was a beautiful box, lacquered dark wood that was inlaid with mother-of-pearl and coral—it was a gift from her parents.

Petra thought of her parents back home as she ran her fingers over the intricate design. She had always kept her finest treasures in this box, *"…just like Kristina's box,"* she smiled in thought. Suddenly, she was inspired. She took the box and carefully removed the contents. She fumbled through her clothes until she found a black velvet muff, thickly lined with soft lamb's wool.

"It's just what I need...now, where's something to..." She groped through her things. *"Here it is,"* she held a small pair of scissors. Petra cut apart the muff and placed one half in the bottom of the box, velvet side down. Then she took the other half and lined the lid of the box. *"That should be soft enough. Now, where is the..."* she took the pickle ornament from the dresser and placed it in the center of the box; nestled in a bed of fine lamb's wool. She closed the lid and latched the box very carefully. *"Perfect. Now, maybe I can rest knowing that it's safe from harm."*

Petra cleared the things off her bed and stretched out across it. Several hours had passed and Petra didn't even realize that she had been sleeping when Kristina came to her room. She had the ornament and all she could think about was getting back to the palace. She wished she could continue sleeping. *"Well, it's dark and you can't leave now. You better freshen up and get dressed for dinner,"* she told herself. *"Besides, maybe you can learn a little more about Master Baumschmuecker and his ornaments. You never know what the King and Queen will ask."*

Dinner was much more intimate than the past few nights. The kitchen had a small rectangular table with a corner bench

seat surrounding two sides, and chairs on the other two. Master Baumschmuecker, Lady Marianne, Kristina, and Petra's Godfather had already taken their seats when Petra entered.

"You get to sit next to me!" Kristina announced as she patted the space next to her on the bench.

Petra smiled and slid in next to Kristina.

"My wife has made our favorite meal tonight: orchard soup and apple-ring pancakes. I hope you'll enjoy the food."

"I'm sure we will," Petra answered. "Tell me a little more about your work, Master Baumschmuecker."

"Please, call me Gustav."

"I heard some of what you told the lady in your workshop. How did you come up with this process?"

"Well, I'm a chemist by trade, but many times I needed glass flasks, jars, and tubes for my work. Glass blowing became almost another trade for me. I soon found it rather relaxing and decided to make a few ornaments and décor for my wife and family."

"What about the silvering process? "

"That also came from my chemistry background. I broke a mirror one day and noticed the blackened backing. I knew how mirrors were made and I just applied the same technique."

Lady Marianne served each a bowl of soup. "This soup is wonderful! It's like having a warm liquid dessert," Petra observed. "There are so many flavors!"

"We have a abundance of orchards here in Klaussendorf. My husband is fond of sweets, so we have sweet dinners three times a week," Marianne said.

"I noticed the orchards as we came into the village. Are most of the people in Klaussendorf orchard growers?"

"No," answered Gustav, "half are, but the other half are mostly doctors, and those dedicated to the study of science."

"Like you and Master Schnellretter?"

"Yes."

Marianne served warm apple-ring pancakes. "These smell divine!" Petra remarked.

"Here's some cinnamon and sugar. Sprinkle it on top," Kristina offered.

"Thank you." Petra tasted her first bite, "Ooooh, I'm in heaven. 'You eat like this three times a week? How lucky you are," she said admiringly.

"Yes, we are lucky," Gustav replied proudly. "Now, why don't you tell us a little about your quest?"

Petra told them all about her journey, what she had seen and whom she had met. Kristina seemed most impressed when she heard about the rare wood-carved figures from Rellischwald, especially the nutcracker. "That nutcracker sounds wonderful. Can we get one, Papa?"

"We'll see, my little pickle," he smiled playfully at Kristina. He turned to Petra and in a more serious tone, continued their conversation. "The different trades and specialties that you have encountered fascinate me. I never knew that we had so many different and talented people in our own Kingdom. Here in Klaussendorf, we get most of our supplies from Dillsburg and we do some trading with Gewurzenbach.

"Really? What do you trade with them?"

"Gewurzenbach has an abundance of streams, lakes, and natural springs—a perfect environment for growing a wide variety of plants, herbs, and spices. We use many of the herbs and plants in our medicines, others we use for flavoring and spicing foods. Gewurzenbach is unique. In the northern part of Gewurzenbach, they have expansive meadows and many of the villagers are expert beekeepers. You must sample some of the many varieties of honey they have to offer: Delicious!"

He paused for a moment and took a sip of wine, " The southern portion is covered with vineyards. The wine we're drinking tonight is from them. It's very good, isn't it?"

"Yes, very. "

"This time of year, they'll have ice wine."

"Ice wine? I've never heard of it."

"It's a specialty. They purposely leave some grapes on the vine to freeze and then they make a wine from it: very, very sweet. You'll have to try that too. That is if you have time—maybe when you stop for lunch tomorrow."

"Yes. Maybe I can purchase a few bottles of wine and some honey to take back with me."

"I think you'll like Gewurzenbach. I haven't been

through there during winter, but the spring and summers are lovely. It's all open spaces and lots of water. They hardly have any trees. We trade our fruits and medical services with them, but we could use more fresh produce and grain up here. I think we should look into the products being offered by the farmers in Heinzinger, as well as some of the services of the other villages."

"You should. I would think they would also like your glass ornaments," Petra added.

Petra was nearly finished eating and she could feel herself becoming anxious again. She fell silent while her Godfather and Gustav engaged in a lengthy discussion about coaches and sleighs. As Petra finished her last bite, she tried to ask off-handedly, "Speaking of our journey, do you know how the weather looks for tomorrow?"

"From what I could tell earlier, it should be clear and sunny. It should be an easy ride back to the palace," Gustav replied.

"Good. I don't think I could take another snowstorm," Petra sighed.

"What's the fastest route back? Should we take the road to Dillsburg?" Petra's Godfather asked.

"Oh, no. It would be best to take the road to Gewurzenbach. It will take you straight through, right to the palace road and you won't have to contend with all the traffic in Dillsburg. Furthermore, the road from here to Dillsburg is in bad repair. Come to think of it, we should look into the services of the stonemason you mentioned from Breinland."

"Petra, would you like something warm to drink before you retire?" Marianne asked.

"No, thank you. You're very kind and dinner was delicious. I think though, I will retire to my room now. I have a very long day ahead of me and I have some things to prepare yet."

"That is certainly understandable," she replied.

Petra kissed her Godfather goodnight, said goodnight to Marianne and Gustav, and then whispered loudly to Kristina, "Can you come with me? I have something for you."

Kristina gave her mother a look to see if she approved, and quickly followed Petra to her room.

"Come in, Kristina. Now, where did I put… Ah, yes—here it is. This is for you," she said, handing Kristina a long cardboard box. "Sit here on the bed and open it."

Kristina grinned and bounded happily on the bed. Her tongue stuck out to the side as she concentrated on untying the  string around the box. She opened the box and unrolled layers and layers of soft paper, "Is it?" she pondered aloud. She unrolled one more layer. "It is! It is!" she cheered jumping up and down. "It's a nutcracker! Oh, he's better than I imagined. Is he mine to keep?"

"Yes, it's my Christmas present to you."

"Thank you," Kristina smiled while playing with the nutcracker's handle. "But I didn't get you anything."

"You already gave me my Christmas gift, and it's the best Christmas gift of all."

"The pickle ornament?"

"No, your friendship. Thank you, Kristina, and Merry Christmas."

"Merry Christmas, Petra."

They hugged, smiled, and kissed each other goodnight. After Kristina left, Petra sat and wrote in her journal. She wrote as much as she could, stored her quill pens and ink in a small pouch, and readied herself for bed. She blew out the candle and lay there staring into darkness for what seemed like hours. In the darkness of night, she imagined what might happen the following day. Some were happy thoughts, while others were nightmares; somewhere in between, she finally fell asleep.

Chapter Eight

*T*he next morning Petra was so excited she could hardly breathe, let alone eat breakfast. They packed their sleigh while it was still somewhat dark. Petra thanked Gustav and Marianne for their hospitality. She then exchanged a tearful goodbye with Kristina, and Petra promised that she would come to see her again. With a snap of the reins, Petra and her Godfather were on their way.

They crept silently through the sleepy streets of the little village and glided for hours through the rolling hills of icy orchards. They passed by the exit to Dillsburg, which looked in disrepair, and sledded smoothly along the road to Gewurzenbach. They road for hours and the sun came full out by midmorning. Petra pulled back the blankets and let the sun warm her. She looked around and as they crossed the first bridge over a river, she knew they must be near Gewurzenbach.

"Gustav was right," she thought in amazement, *"the fields go on forever. Not a mountain, hill, or even a tree in sight."*

Over the next several hours, they crossed over a dozen bridges spanning a variety of streams, brooks, creeks, and rivulets. Petra found herself gritting her teeth and holding her breath out of fear that a bridge may collapse every time they crossed one. Most of the wood tresses creaked and moaned, but some even bowed and swayed. Though the bridges and waterways were the only break in the expansive whiteness of the scenery, it seemed that the region went on forever without an edge.

It was early afternoon, when Petra noticed a large shining lake and a small community clustered at its edge. "Is that Gewurzenbach?" Petra asked her Godfather.

"Part of it. I think we'll stop there, find an Inn, rest, and get something to eat before we continue."

"Sounds good! How are we doing? Do you think we'll get to the palace in time?" she asked anxiously.

"I don't think we'll have a problem. We should get there before nightfall."

It was another half-hour before they reached an Inn by the lake. The Inn was spacious, warm, and bright. The Innkeeper, a handsome looking gentleman named Master Wiesenblatt, seated Petra and her Godfather at a table next to a large window over-looking the lake.

The view was breathtaking. The lake was smooth as glass, and glistened and sparkled in the afternoon sun. Petra could see the reflection of the sky in the lake and at a distance; it was difficult to tell the difference between reality and the reflection. She marveled at the sight.

"It's magnificent!" Petra exclaimed.

"You should see it in spring. With everything in bloom, it's spectacular," Master Wiesenblatt replied. "What would you like? Something warm to drink or something to eat perhaps?"

"A little of both. What are your specialties?" Petra asked.

"I suggest a hot Cinna-mint tea to drink."

"Cinna-mint?"

"Yes, it's a combination of peppermint, comfrey, and

alfalfa tea spiced with cloves and a stick of Cinnamon, and sweetened with a touch of honey. 'Very soothing on a cold winter's day."

Petra and her Godfather both nodded while Master Wiesenblatt continued, "For a hot and satisfying lunch, I suggest our sweet-and-sour cabbage soup with a side of potato dumplings."

"What's in the soup besides cabbage?" asked Petra's Godfather.

"Sliced leeks and a few carrots. We season it with onions, garlic, and thyme; and we add a little wine vinegar and honey for the sweet and sour taste."

"That sounds wonderful! I'm famished," Petra's Godfather exclaimed.

The meal was warm and satisfying, as promised, and Petra was delighted to find that the meal also included warm bread rolls and several ramekins of different flavored honey. She sampled every one of them—the lavender honey was among her favorites.

When Master Wiesenblatt returned to their table Petra asked, "Can we purchase jars of these honeys? I just love the lavender flavored, but I also like the jasmine and the rosemary. We were told that honey is a specialty in Gewurzenbach, but I never imagined that there would be such a difference in flavors."

"The different flavors depend on the type of flowers that the bees visit. Each beekeeper lives in a different area of Gewurzenbach, where a different field and combination of plants grow. The honey is available in pints. Which ones would you like?"

"I would like to take one of each—except the lavender. I'd like two pints of that one. In addition, do you have ice wine? We've heard wonderful things about the wine and we would like to try it."

"I'm sorry, Mistress. We don't have any at this time. Ice wine is the specialty of Southern Gewurzenbach, the heart of which is approximately three hours from here."

"Southern Gewurzenbach?"

"Yes. You see Gewurzenbach is actually made up of two smaller villages. Northern Gewurzenbach, where you are now, is on a lake surrounded by meadows. Our specialty up here is herbs, spices, flowers, and honey—lots of honey. Southern Gewurzenbach is made up of vineyards. Their specialties are grapes and grape products such as wine, vinegar, raisins, and jellies."

"Why two smaller villages?"

"Just a matter of convenience. Our properties are very large and divided by crisscrossing rivers and streams. Sometimes bridges are a problem, which makes traveling difficult. We found that having two smaller villages made it easier."

Petra and her Godfather paid for their meals and the jars of honey and were on their way again. After two hours on the road, Petra noticed that the scenery was changing. There were more hills and she noticed that there were homes tucked in at the base of some them. "Godfather! Those must be the vineyards. Do you think we can stop in Southern Gewurzenbach?"

"I was planning to—we're doing fine time-wise and we could use a little break to stretch our legs."

Petra was feeling quite content. She was warm and happy. She took her journal in hand and flipped through the pages, rereading her entries. *"Has it really only been five days?"* she thought in amazement. Just then, they crossed another bridge. It shuddered beneath the weight of the horses and sleigh.

Petra tucked her journal back in her bag and clung on to the seat. As they made it safely across, she had a passing thought, "They should get Masters Holzfaeller and Schnitzelmeier over here to build their bridges. They have the lumber and the skills." With that thought, she decided that at the next stop she should make a few more entries in her journal.

It was another hour before they made it to the heart of Southern Gewurzenbach. It was a pleasant little village surrounded by rolling hills of snow-covered vineyards.

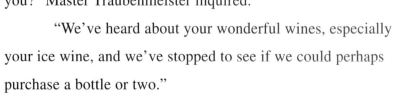

At the Inn where they stopped, Master Traubenmeister and his wife Gertrude greeted them very warmly.

"Merry Christmas travelers! Come in and warm yourselves by the fire. How may we help you?" Master Traubenmeister inquired.

"We've heard about your wonderful wines, especially your ice wine, and we've stopped to see if we could perhaps purchase a bottle or two."

"Well, it's nice to know that you've heard good things about our wine. Although, before you purchase, you must first taste. Please be our guests, have a seat, and sample some of our best," Master Traubenmeister replied.

"Thank you. We cannot stay long—we're somewhat pressed for time."

"Yes. Yes. That's understandable. After all, it is Christmas Eve," Gertrude commented as she served them several small glasses. In each glass, she poured a sip or two of wine. She also brought them a platter with bread. "In between sips, eat some bread to cleanse your palette. It will help you distinguish the tastes."

"Thank you."

The wine tasting was very enlightening. Master Traubenmeister and Gertrude pointed out some of the subtleties in each of the wines and taught them which wines are best with different foods.

Petra loved the ice wine. While her Godfather arranged to purchase several different bottles of wine, Petra sat at a table sipping a small glass of the sweet ice wine while she wrote in her journal.

When her Godfather was finished loading the sleigh, she closed her book, took one last sip, and stood to leave. "Do you know how much further it is to the palace from here?" she asked as she headed out the door.

"About one-and-a-half hours," answered Master Traubenmeister. "About a half-hour from here you'll enter a valley where you'll cross the last river, from there it's less than an hour's ride to the palace."

"Wonderful! Thank you so much for your hospitality. I'm sure we'll be back and I will tell my family and friends. Merry Christmas!"

"Merry Christmas and safe travels," they called in unison.

In the sleigh once more, the half hour passed quickly. It was very late in the afternoon and the sky was beginning to change into its evening colors. As they slid into the valley, she looked up. "Look, Godfather! The palace! I can see it from here!"

"Yes. I see it. However, there's something up ahead. It looks as though something has happened at the bridge."

"What?"

As they approached the bridge, a

man ran toward them waving his hands. "Wait! Stop! The bridge is out!" he shouted.

Petra's Godfather pulled hard on the reins, "Whoa! Whoa!" he called to the horses and pulled hard to bring them to a stop. "What happened?"

"The bridge collapsed about two hours ago. We had to rescue a couple of people, their horses, and wagon. The bridge has completely collapsed. It will be days before it's repaired."

"Where's the alternative crossing? We must cross to get to the palace," Petra's Godfather said with a tone of importance.

"The only other crossing is back toward Northern Gewurzenbach. About three hours back. You can cross into Gurkenheim there."

"Three hours! That's not possible! We must cross here. Isn't there any other way?" Petra pleaded in desperation.

115

"We have a small ferry. We can only take people; your horses and sleigh cannot cross. The ferry is too small and the water is too swift and cold."

"Are there horses and a sleigh or carriage available across the river?" Petra's Godfather asked.

"Not a sleigh or carriage," a young man answered, "but I live over there and I have a horse I could spare."

"I'll take it!" Petra cried. "Godfather, you take the sleigh back into Gurkenheim and meet me later at the palace. I'll continue alone on horseback.

"Petra! You can't!"

"It's less than an hour away. I can see the palace from here. I must make it before nightfall or I'll be disqualified."

"You don't even know how to ride!"

Petra jumped from the carriage, "Can you teach me how to ride well enough so that I can make it to the palace?"

The young man looked bewildered and stammered, "Well, yes…I suppose so, Mistress. But…"

Before he could finish Petra interrupted, "Excellent! Then I'm off. Godfather, I'll see you later."

"Petra. I don't like this. You'll be without an escort."

"I don't have a choice. It must be so. Please, let me do

it this way. Trust me. I'll be fine." She grabbed her bag that contained her journal and the treasure box that held her glass ornament.

Her Godfather had gotten down from the sleigh to help her. "Let me come with you across the river. We'll have someone watch the horses and sleigh. I'll stay with you until you leave."

Petra took a deep breath. "Let's go then."

They arranged for someone to care for the horses and the sleigh and followed the young man onto a ferry. Petra clutched her bag tightly and watched as one ferryman used a large staff to push off from the riverbank, while two other men used their brut strength to pull the ferry across the river by means of a rope suspended from one side of the river to the other.

When they arrived on the other side of the river, Petra and her Godfather thanked the ferrymen and quickly followed the young man to his house.

"I'm sorry," Petra apologized. "You've been so kind and we haven't introduced ourselves. I'm Petra, daughter of Sir Nicholas and Lady Karolina; and this is my Godfather, Sir Arthur."

"Mistress Petra," the young man bowed. "I am Master Gutmann." Master Gutmann's house was a small house at the river's edge. He had only two horses in his stable. "This is the

horse you can ride. She's smaller, well behaved, and should be easy for you to handle. Her name's Sophia."

"Well, hello there Sophia," Petra said as she petted her.

"Let me saddle her. Then I'll teach you what you need to know to ride." Master Gutmann grabbed a saddle and slung it on to Sophia's back.

"Wait a minute," Petra's Godfather waved his hands. "That's a regular saddle. She'll need a sidesaddle. After all, she's a lady."

"I'm sorry. This is the only type of saddle I have."

"Petra, riding by yourself is bad enough, but to ride like a man..."

Petra bit her lower lip, "Is it more difficult this way?" she asked Master Gutmann.

"More difficult?"

"Yes. Is it more difficult to ride this way than riding side-saddle?"

"I don't know, Mistress. I've never ridden side-saddle," he blushed, "but I would think that it is easier riding this way; straddling the horse. You'll have more control."

"More control? Then it's safer to ride this way?"

Master Gutmann looked at Petra's Godfather and hesitated to reply, but then he saw the defeated look on her Godfather's face and answered, "Yes, I guess it is."

"Good. Then I'll ride this way. Now, let's get to the lesson."

Master Gutmann finished saddling Sophia and packed Petra's things in the saddlebags. He showed her how to mount and dismount the horse; how to get Sophia to walk, trot, and gallop; how to turn; how to stop, and most importantly, how to stay on the horse.

Sophia was a good-natured and patient horse, which helped Petra learn very quickly and helped her feel at ease.

"I think I've got it now…at least well enough to make it to the palace," Petra said as she came galloping back from a practice run. "Daylight is fading fast. I must be on my way."

Remaining in her saddle, Petra bent down to kiss her Godfather, "Don't worry about me."

"Be careful, Petra," her Godfather told her with concern.

"You, too. I'll see you tonight!" She turned Sophia around, "Thank you for everything, Master Gutmann. I'll make sure to return Sophia to you as soon as possible. Merry Christmas!" she called over her shoulder as she road off in a gallop toward the palace.

Petra had never felt such freedom. Riding Sophia was exhilarating. The wind whipped at her face and hair as they galloped up the palace road. The sun was setting and the shadows grew longer. She could feel Sophia breathing hard beneath her and she could see the puffs of air billowing from her flared nostrils. "Good girl. Keep going, we're almost there," she called soothingly to Sophia.

As they neared the palace, Petra couldn't help imagining what someone might say as she entered the palace on horseback; riding as a man would. She almost hoped someone she knew would see her. She felt strangely independent and empowered. They approached the gate just as

darkness began to settle over the Kingdom of Vlassika. "We made it," Petra whispered to Sophia, "just in time."

Petra trotted Sophia over to the palace stables where the stable boy, Gerhart met her. "Mistress Petra?" he asked in disbelief.

"Yes. I have no time to explain," she said as she dismounted without assistance. "Please take good care of her. Her name is Sophia. I'll give you instructions as to where to bring her tomorrow."

"Yes, Mistress."

Petra unpacked her saddlebags. "I'm sorry...I'm late and I must hurry to dress. Merry Christmas, Gerhart!"

"Merry Christmas, Mistress!"

Petra clutched her bag closely and rushed inside. She ran up the stairs and knocked on her Governess's door. "It's Petra. I'm back!"

The door flung open, "Petra! Oh, I was so worried," her Governess cried as she hugged her.

"There's not much time. I need your help to get ready."

"Yes. I see that. And you…smell like a …a…" she wrinkled her nose, "a horse?"

"It's a long story. We'll talk while I get ready."

Petra's Governess called for a few handmaidens and they all went to Petra's quarters to assist her. With their help, they had Petra bathed, perfumed, beautifully dressed, and impeccably coifed in record time.

While she bathed, Petra told her Governess and the handmaidens some of what she had experienced. While having her hair styled, Petra checked to ensure the glass ornament was not broken. Before slipping into her dress, she also made a few last entries in her journal.

She was perfumed and powdered, and then dressed. As a final addition, one of the handmaidens placed a wreath of flowers to crown her hair, while another pinned a brooch to the bodice of her dress. Petra stood before her Governess and twirled slowly in her gold brocade gown. Her long dark tresses looked like velvet against her powdered white skin.

"How do I look?" she asked.

"You look like a princess… like a princess," her Governess sighed with tears in her eyes.

Petra blushed and smiled, "Well, then I had better go." Petra took a deep breath, "I don't know if I can do this."

"After all that you've accomplished, this will be the easy part," her Governess comforted.

Petra smiled proudly, "I guess you're right."

Chapter Nine

*P*etra entered the great hall carrying her journal and the object of her quest: the glass ornament, still safely tucked inside the lacquered box. It was very crowded. Everyone seemed to be there: the contestants, their escorts, friends, and family; courtiers; court officials from across the Kingdom; and noblemen and noblewomen of every rank. Petra stood at the edges of the crowd and peered on tiptoe. She was looking for her parents, but she couldn't see them—there were just too many people and too many hats!

They were all dressed in their best holiday clothing and the contestants all clung tightly to boxes that Petra knew were glass ornaments from Master Baumschmuecker. She noticed that the King and Queen had not yet arrived. Their thrones stood empty next to the palace Christmas tree, which the staff had sparingly decorated with glittered pinecones, gingerbread rings, foil-wrapped chocolates, and butter cookies bejeweled with multicolored candy sprinkles. She could see that they had clipped candles to each tiny branch, but that the candles remained unlit. Several attendants stood at attention near the tree holding the staffs and ladders that would allow them to light the candles and (she supposed) to hang the glass ornaments on the tree.

As she looked around the grand room, in the crowd she recognized a friendly face; with a broad smile, he approached her.

"Sir Manfred!" she exclaimed with joy. "What a pleasure it is to see you," she curtsied with grace.

"The pleasure is all mine!" Sir Manfred bowed and took her hand, "You look like a princess," he whispered as he kissed her hand and looked into her eyes.

Petra blushed, from not only his gaze, but also his words. They were the same that her Governess had spoken. She calmed herself and quickly regained her composure. "Thank you."

"I'm so happy see that you have made it back safely. I was worried. I inquired about you several times, and I was told you had not yet returned."

"Yes, well. I returned this evening. It was quite an adventure for me."

"Not everyone made it back. That is to say, not everyone is still in the contest. Some were not able to find the ornament maker and a few were disqualified. One contestant was disqualified for stealing a carriage—remember the young doctor and his wife in Dillsburg?"

"Their carriage?"

"Yes. After they told him where the ornament maker lives, he felt that he couldn't get to his horse fast enough, so he stole their carriage! He was found out and disqualified."

"Serves him right! What an awful thing to do! They were on a medical mission. That could have cost some people their lives!" Petra thought about that day in Dillsburg and paused in thought, "So, is that why you were smiling so broadly when I last saw you in Dillsburg? You had found out…"

"You too, I assumed. I even waited an extra day in Klaussendorf in hopes to see you. When you didn't arrive, I was a bit concerned. What happened?"

"It's a long story. I had quite an adventure. As I said they were…" a sudden blaring of trumpets announcing the entrance of the King and Queen interrupted Petra.

The great hall fell silent except for the rustling of taffeta gowns and the jingling of metal swords as everyone bowed and curtsied in respect.

King Frederick's voice boomed across the hall, "Merry Christmas and Welcome! It's so wonderful to see all of you again! I know you're all anxious to see and hear what our eager contestants

have brought back with them. So let us begin immediately.
When the registrar calls your name, please come forward and
present yourself. Present your ornament for the palace tree and
be prepared to tell us what you have learned and experienced on
your quest." The King paused while Queen Margarete took a
seat on her throne. "Registrar!"

The registrar came forward and bowed before King
Frederick.

"Open your book and call the first contestant."

One-by-one the contestants presented themselves. Petra
was astonished at the wonderful ornaments that each presented to
the royal couple. Each ornament was as fantastic as the next.
There were large swirling, vibrant bubbles of glass, and a variety
of fanciful shapes—sparkling with every color imaginable.
Some of the pieces were as large as a child's head.

With each presentation, Petra's spirits sank lower and lower. She caressed the box that held her ornament and thought in shame, *"What am I going to do? I can't possibly present this ornament to the King and Queen!"* She was nearly in tears. Her throat tightened. She wanted to turn and run, but her legs wouldn't move. Then she remembered her promise to Kristina. Kristina had given her this ornament out of friendship and compassion.

She calmed herself with these thoughts and began to listen more carefully to the contestants. They all seemed nearly the same. Almost all of the contestants had stayed in Dillsburg. They talked about different Inns, how comfortable the beds were, and which served the best ale. Most of them didn't know anything about the ornament maker or the process that he used to make the ornaments. When they discovered where the ornament maker lived, they headed straight for Klaussendorf, and in most cases, headed right back to Dillsburg for the night.

Sir Manfred was one of the only contestants who had stopped in Gurkenheim and spent time in Klaussendorf. The ornament he presented to King Frederick and Queen Margarete was spectacular. It was nearly two feet long and contained three bubbles of glass, graduating in size from large to small and ending with a tall swirling spike.

There were indents on the sides of each bubble, "These indentations are called reflectors," he explained as he turned the ornament to catch the light, casting tiny rainbows across the great hall. "Master Baumschmuecker, the ornament maker, said that he calls this ornament a finial, because it's meant to adorn the very top of the tree." Everyone was impressed, especially King Frederick and Queen Margarete.

Petra's stomach churned as she heard each of the following contestants and she realized that she would soon make her presentation. Every time she started to get nervous, she thought about how far she had come and all that she had accomplished. She inwardly practiced what she would say.

Abruptly, the registrar interrupted her silent rehearsal, "Mistress Petra, daughter of Sir Nicholas and Lady Karolina—Royal sponsor: her Majesty, Queen Margarete."

Petra took a deep breath and strode forward; she curtsied deeply before King Frederick and Queen Margarete. She was stunned at how quiet it had become. She could hear herself breathing.

"Rise and present your ornament," King Frederick commanded in a friendly tone.

Petra rose and held out the lacquered box with one hand, "For your royal Majesties and the palace Christmas tree," Petra said formally.

King Frederick took the box, "What a handsome box!" he said admiringly, "Now, for the treasure inside." He sat on his throne as he carefully opened the box. His face took on a surprised expression, which he quickly suppressed. He gingerly removed the little ornament from its cozy refuge. "My what an interesting ornament," King Frederick said as he held the ornament up for view.

A wave of mutters and snickers circulated through the hall.

"It's a...?" King Frederick looked briefly at Queen Margarete for help, then at Petra.

"It's a pickle, your Majesty," Petra answered boldly.

Laughter rang throughout. King Frederick stood and waved his hand to subdue the laughter. "Tell me, Mistress Petra. How did you come to choose this particular ornament?" he asked.

"Your Highness, I did not as much choose this ornament, as it chose me."

"That's an odd answer. Can you explain yourself?"

"Yes. But if your Majesty will allow, I would also like to present you with this," Petra held out her journal, "to accompany the ornament I have given you."

King Frederick handed the pickle ornament to Queen Margarete and accepted the journal from Petra. "Thank you. What is it?" King Frederick asked as he took a seat on his throne and began looking through it.

"It's my journal. I made notes recording all what I have observed and learned while on my quest. It will explain in great detail how I came to present this very special ornament."

"I see. This is quite detailed—maps, drawings…now, tell us some of what this contains."

Petra began telling the tale of her journey. As she told her story, the great hall became quiet. There were occasional sounds of awe, such as when she told them about the methods that the people of Rellischwald use to ward off bears. As she continued, King

Frederick paged through her journal, occasionally asking questions.

"You've made many notes here. What is this about the stone masons and the road in Gurkenheim?" King Frederick asked.

Petra explained how she thought several of the villages would benefit from exchanging goods and services. She pointed out that she made many specific notes on the strengths and weakness of each village she encountered and how she thought they could correct things with the aid or products from another village within the Kingdom.

The crowd listened attentively. Petra told of her arrival in Klaussendorf and she nearly moved them all to tears when she told of Kristina's great act of kindness and the promise that she had made her. Queen Margarete sniffled as she held the precious little pickle ornament in her hand. She dabbed her eyes and looked with wonder as Petra explained the process that Master Baumschmuecker used to make his glass ornaments.

As Petra told of her final approach to the palace and her horseback ride to the palace grounds, the hall filled with cheers as they reveled in her accomplishment.

"Your Highness," Petra said, "this little ornament may seem small and insignificant, but it is very special. It represents my journey—all that I have observed and learned in only five days. It not only represents the kindness and generosity of a small child, but it represents the kindness, generosity, strength, wisdom, and talents of all the people I have met these last few days." Petra paused and then continued, "To me this ornament represents the Kingdom of Vlassika—a great Kingdom made up of villages (large and small); neighborhoods; families; and most

importantly, individuals. An individual may seem small and insignificant as compared to a Kingdom, but it is the individual who makes the bread; farms the land; builds the fences, bridges, and roads; herds the sheep; cures the ill; and makes this Kingdom great."

Silence hung over the great hall. Someone clapping his hands together broke the silence. Petra glanced toward the audience and saw that it was Sir Manfred. He held his head high, smiling while he clapped approvingly. Within seconds, more people joined in and started clapping until the entire hall filled with applause.

King Frederick stood. As the room quieted he said, "This ornament is special, indeed! I will always treasure it. Thank you very much, Mistress Petra."

With a small curtsy, Petra silently stepped back into the crowd. Her heart was pounding and her mouth was dry, but she had done her best. *"At least I didn't make a fool of myself,"* she thought in consolation.

King Frederick and Queen Margarete whispered quietly before he began again. "Now, regarding the reason we have all gathered here," King Frederick spoke in a serious tone. "As we had hoped," he paused and looked to Queen Margarete who smiled and nodded slightly, "we have found someone who is worthy of being crowned as heir to our throne. All of you have done a wonderful job, but there is one among you who is assuredly outstanding…"

Petra looked to where Sir Manfred was standing, caught his eye, and smiled at him. *"He'd make a fine King,"* she mused.

King Frederick was still speaking and Petra tried to clear her thoughts so that she could listen. Her mind was racing and she couldn't focus. She heard only bits and pieces—a few phrases.

"Compassion and understanding…"

She imagined how Sir Manfred would look crowned as Prince and heir to the throne.

"Must know the people, their needs, and concerns…"

Petra glanced at Sir Manfred again and quickly looked away when she noticed he was looking at her. She blushed and tried to look elsewhere.

"Must possess the ability to listen, learn, observe, and assess every situation, while obtaining the best for all concerned…"

Petra tried to look across the way at someone else, but when she did, it seemed they were looking at her. Her face burned with embarrassment. *"Why are they looking at me?"* she thought self-conscientiously.

"We have all seen those qualities here tonight in one person. I present to you our heir to the throne…"

Petra quietly instructed herself, *"Smile and be happy. Don't look disappointed. He'll make a wonderful Prince and King."*

"Princess Petra!"

Cries of joy, cheers of adoration, and applause filled the great hall. King Frederick held out his hand to Petra. She was stunned. She couldn't move.

Tears streamed down her cheeks as she looked to King Frederick and Queen Margarete in confusion. Queen Margarete came to her and hugged her, whispering, "Congratulations, Petra. I'm very proud of you."

Petra muttered a heartfelt, "Thank you."

As Queen Margarete let go, behind her was a throng of people waiting to congratulate Princess Petra: her parents, Governess, Sir Manfred, friends, family, and even her Godfather, who had returned just in time to see her presentation.

In the midst of the celebration, King Frederick raised his hands once more to speak. The great hall fell silent in respect. "In honor of Princess Petra," King Frederick declared, "the palace Christmas tree shall always include a Christmas Pickle! It shall always be the last ornament to be placed on the tree—hidden where only the most observant can find it."

Everyone laughed and applauded. King Frederick personally hung the Christmas Pickle on the palace tree and announced with great joy, "Light the tree and let us rejoice on this very special Christmas Eve!"

Chapter Ten

The jubilation continued through the Twelve Days of Christmas, ending with the official coronation on Epiphany. Petra invited all of her family and friends, including the new friends that she had made during her very special journey.

Petra was particularly happy to see Kristina. Petra showed her the palace Christmas tree and told her of King Frederick's proclamation. Kristina was very impressed that her friend had become a Princess and she danced with joy when Petra told her that she would always be welcome in the palace as a royal guest.

After the festivities of the coronation, Petra went to work. She was attentive and studied hard to learn what she needed to know. She traveled frequently and visited all the villages of the

Kingdom of Vlassika—observing, listening, and becoming acquainted with the people that she would some day serve.

The villagers loved Princess Petra and often affectionately referred to her as the "Pickle Princess." Through the years, the people grew to cherish Princess Petra even more. They celebrated with great fanfare, her marriage to Sir Manfred and rejoiced at the birth of their children. Their admiration and devotion was so great that most of the villagers adopted the custom of the Christmas Pickle as a part of their own Christmas traditions. Every Christmas Eve, the little children of Vlassika would clamber to find the hidden Christmas Pickle—to receive a special gift and be crowned Prince or Princess of the day as the most observant in all the land.

When the time came, Queen Petra reigned with extraordinary wisdom and grace, and the Kingdom of Vlassika flourished in every way. The people of surrounding Kingdoms came to admire Vlassika for their exceptional products and fine craftsmanship.

However, to this day, the grand Kingdom of Vlassika is foremost renowned as the origin of the "Christmas Pickle."

The Tradition of the Christmas Pickle

On Christmas Eve,

The Christmas Pickle is the very last ornament

To be placed on the Christmas tree –

Hidden deep

Within the tree's branches.

Upon viewing of the tree,

The boy or girl who first finds the

Christmas Pickle receives a special gift and is

Crowned Prince or Princess of the day

In honor of being

The most observant

In all the land.

Photo by Marianne Beams DeLuca

Judy Lee Aguiar

Judy (Maasch) Aguiar was born in Phoenix, Arizona. Her parents, Arthur and Margrit Maasch and her sister, Janny, were born in Germany. Judy grew up as a first generation American—speaking two languages and trying to cling to the roots of her German heritage that was rich with old world customs and traditions.

Judy has lived most of her life in Arizona, but during two years in high school, she did live in Karlsruhe, Germany (her family's hometown). It was in Karlsruhe where Judy experienced her first "White Christmas," complete with ringing church bells at midnight—quite a contrast to the "Original Christmas" of Arizona with sand and palm trees.

In addition to being a writer, Judy Aguiar is the owner of The European Christmas Market in Scottsdale, Arizona—making her well known in the community as an authority on Christmas traditions.

She has made numerous special appearances on the local news channels, providing Christmas decorating tips and ideas. She has also been the subject of many statewide newspaper articles regarding traditions of Christmas and decorating for the holidays.

In addition, Judy participated as an expert on Christmas traditions and symbols in a nationwide curriculum broadcast for Elementary schools as presented by Prentice-Hall, Inc. and the Educational Management Group.

Judy also developed and maintains a large Christmas website, www.europeanchristmas.com, that is complete with links to Christmas symbols, traditions, carols, recipes, and Holiday activities for all ages.

Judy's childhood memories are overflowing with old-fashioned, German Christmas traditions. Her husband, Manuel Aguiar is an American of Latin descent, with a large family—there is an abundance of love, lots of children, and their Christmas celebrations always center on plenty of delectable food specialties.

In their household, Judy and Manuel try to blend their ethnic backgrounds to create a warm, loving mix of family and tradition. They and their families celebrate Christmas over a month-long period—beginning with opening of the first window of the Advent Calendar and ending with Epiphany on January 6.

Santa Claus comes to their house on December 6, bringing German chocolates, nuts, fruits, and the German Lebkuchen (gingerbread) from Nürnberg in it's decorated tin. Tamales (with a black olive in the center) are steamed and served all month and everyone always eats Nana's empanadas (pumpkin turnovers) before they even get a chance to cool.

Judy and Manuel decorate the Christmas tree with tiny white and colored lights, fresh baby's breath, and European glass ornaments—including the Christmas Pickle! They light the candles of an Advent Wreath in observance of the four Sundays of Advent, and celebrate Christmas on Christmas Eve with the coming of the Christkind (Christ Child Angel). Before they open any gifts, they always sing Christmas carols in German and in English, and they never take down the Christmas tree until after Epiphany. Judy and Manuel soon hope to have a child, which will make their Christmas celebration even more special as seen in the reflection of their child's eyes.

Currently, aside from operating and managing The European Christmas Market and her website, Judy is busy writing several additional books. Two books are being prepared for publication in 2003. Be sure to look for them:

- *The Littlest Camel*, a Christmas story that takes you on an adventure through the 12 days of Christmas.

- *The Heavenly Plan*, a story in verse that explains how Guardian angels are able to watch over every one of us.